The Anthropologist

Jon Ferguson

Huge Jam Publishing
2022

First published in the UK
by Huge Jam, 2022

ISBN: 978-1-911249-97-9

1

March 1999

Fuller sat on the desk and watched the last students trickle out the door. He observed, for the umpteenth time, the balancing act of the absurdly oversized jeans hanging across the middle of most of the male butts (to his surprise, he had still never seen a pair fall to the floor) and the girls' bare midriffs bounce-floating above their jeans that seemed glued to the widest part of their hips. He knew a few names, but not many. It was an *Anthro Intro 101* class and there were about sixty pupils. He had noticed years before that the older he got the fewer students hung around him after a lecture, especially the females. On this day a handful said goodbye, but no one made a move in his direction. Class ended at four; by four-oh-two the room was empty except for himself, the desks, and the chairs.

To try to wake up the group of bobbing afternoon heads, he had closed out his discourse with an anecdote about an African tribe where the witch doctor cuts off the head of a chicken, analyzes the pattern of the blood that has squirted on the ground between himself and the patient, then, on that basis, solves whatever problem the person sitting in front of him might have. It seems to work quite well. The doctor's powers are rarely, if ever, questioned. Fuller had heard the story when he was a student thirty-odd years prior. He couldn't remember the name of the tribe – the "Arunti" or Ashunti" or whatever – but he didn't care. He hadn't and wouldn't bother to look it up. The story had stayed stored in some soft corner of his noggin. The teacher's name, however, he remembered: Dr. Merlin Myers, a Chicago School man. It was Myers more than anyone else who had pushed Fuller into the field of Cultural Anthropology. Images like the miniature geyser of chicken blood falling on the dirt inside an African hut had always taken his mind off the war in Vietnam and sex for a while. His junior year he switched his major from engineering to anthropology. Dr. Myers liked his senior thesis, "Symbolic Reality: A Socio-Anthropological Essay on the Nature of Reality" and nudged him into following his tracks to Chicago to do his doctorate. That was in 1969.

"Strap-on, 69ers," he thought as he picked up his battered briefcase. He hadn't heard this expression since his freshman year in high school. When he heard it then, mostly coming out of the mouths of football players or guys that were trying to look like Elvis, he didn't know what it meant. He turned off the light and walked out into the spring air. He often wondered why he still carried the briefcase to classes because he almost never opened it. His lectures were like rocks rubbed smooth and slick by the flow of eons of water. In this case the eons were twenty-five years of teaching the same crap. Three decades of anthropology had essentially done one thing to Fuller: it had made him lose respect for the human race. This isn't wholly correct. He had lost respect for man as a "free" being, but still had great respect for what man was able to make. On the one hand, man was a slave, but on the other hand he was a great builder.

The campus for example. It was beautiful and beautifully kept up by a team of gardeners that Fuller admired as much or more than his fellow professors. Most of the gardeners were Mexicans who likely hadn't had many breaks in life, but who mowed lawns, trimmed trees and planted flowers with wonderful results. Fuller always held his small seminars outside when the weather permitted. He figured that if he and the students were boring each other, at least they all had the landscape and the sky to look at. He only knew one of the school gardeners by name, Juan José Carlos Rodriguez. He looked to be long past retirement age, but because he had come into the country with wet feet and no passport, he had probably invented an age that had allowed him to work well into his seventies. Fuller had once asked him how old he was and he had laughed and said, "Old enough to know I don't be planting fucking flores forever." Over the years Fuller had invited him into his office on a number of occasions for a hot or a cold drink.

It was warm out and Fuller took off his jacket and held it over his left shoulder with a finger. He asked himself why he still wore a sports jacket to teach in. He decided it must be the pockets and he had to wear something. The Anthropology Department was at the extreme south end of campus. Fuller lived on the north side, but he enjoyed the walk. He wandered toward the student union building and decided to go in for a cup of coffee. He had papers to correct that evening, maybe. He sat down at a table next to a couple that were touching fingers and staring like owls into each other's eyes. Strap on, 69ers. Anthropology had taught him another thing: in most societies, the guys in power are, one way or another, usually sexually very active. How often had he studied tribes in which the chief *had to* deflower all the virgins before they were passed on to their husbands? Often. Or tribes in which the chief's list of wives was as long as a Denny's menu? Often. Was Western civilization an exception? wondered he more than once. Openly, yes. Behind closed doors it was hard to know. Kennedy had shacked up with quite a few evidently. But had Nixon? Had Gerald Ford? Jimmy Carter? Certainly not Carter. He felt guilty just thinking about a substitute for Rosalyn. Reagan? Hard to say. Nancy seemed like she kept those handcuffs on pretty tight. Clinton? Probably not nearly as much as he hoped for. Too many eyes on the White House. Who knows? The French and Italians seem to wield a different stick. Mitterand's mistress sat next to his wife at his funeral. Chirac and Berlusconi look like they're doing their face-lifts to capture more than votes.

Fuller dropped a sugar cube into his coffee. The couple were now leaning over the table kissing. One of them knocked a glass on the floor which brought the embrace to an end. Serves them right, Fuller thought only meaning it halfheartedly. He was all for love. What bothered him was that in spite of the risks that seemed to pop up every decade or so, it seemed like this young generation was getting it on like rabbits. MTV made the youth culture look like a non-stop merry-go-round orgy. When he was a kid they carried chewing gum and Certs in their pockets; these kids carry ten-packs of rubbers.

The boy and girl were picking up the pieces of the broken glass. Fuller noticed that a G-string, sliding purposely above the girl's pants, looked like it was made of see-through plastic. Plastic underwear? Is this possible? But they did have those plastic brassiere straps. At least, they looked plastic. When they were back in their chairs, Fuller considered asking the girl what her undergarments were made of, but they never made eye contact. Fuller noticed that eye contact and age were inversely proportional: the older you became the less people looked at you. He still tried, tried all the time, but now that he was in his late fifties, the only people who looked at him were people trying to sell him something or doctors and dentists. *Fucking flores*, he thought.

Fuller's second wife had died along with their Toyota

minivan five years earlier. They, wife and minivan, hit a tree – a tree hit them – one night while they were coming home from her aerobics class. A patch of ice was deemed responsible for bringing the three together. So the police said, anyway. Fuller had been devastated at the moment, but later realized that maybe people over fifty are better off living alone. They had been married for six years, and after the honeymoon had ended, he had felt he was in his wife's way most of the time. Her incessant complaints about his dirty shoes, toothpaste marks in the basin, rings around the bathtub, and poorly-scoured pots and pans all ceased with her death. Though he never made it public, he secretly concluded that their separation had been a good thing. He just wished it had come about more peacefully.

His first wife, with whom he had lovely twin daughters, moved in with her psychiatrist the day after her daughters went away to college. Fuller remembered, September 1st, 1984. They had agreed to stay together until the girls were gone. Dolores wasted not a day. On September 2nd she loaded the Saab with three suitcases and a duffel bag and drove three miles to Dr. Arthur Barnes's apartment and scotch-taped her name under his on the mailbox. Sixteen months later the mailbox said "Dr. and Mrs. Dolores Barnes". Fuller couldn't have been happier. His wife had somebody to talk to and the psychiatrist had somebody to screw. Every now and then it was the other way around. So Dolores said anyway.

Fuller still lived in the house he and Dolores had bought when he got the job at the university. Dolores always complained that it was his job that decided where they lived and not hers. She had been a pregnant fashion designer then. Fuller had no beef about following her to New York or Los Angeles or wherever fashion gets fabricated, but she had quit her job with a difficult pregnancy while Fuller was offered a full-time position on a Colorado campus. They moved from Chicago to the foot of the Rockies. Dolores became an interior decorator.

When Fuller opened the door the radio was on. He never locked the house using an anthropologist's reverse psychology that if the door is locked and the thieves don't get an answer when they ring the doorbell, they'll rob the place; if the door is open they'll think somebody is home and they'll go rob somebody else. Besides, there was nothing to steal anyway. His TV barely worked, he didn't have a computer or a DVD player, his paintings were abstract, his clothes were mostly bought twenty years ago, his music system was a turntable and bulky speakers, and he didn't wear jewelry. Fuller wondered why the radio, his clock-radio (the only radio in the house), was on. He turned it off and looked at the bedding. Were the sheets and blankets the way he left them that morning? He never made the bed before he went to work. He didn't know how he had left things. He pulled up the covers, bent over, and put his nose to the sheets to see if he could detect a foreign odor, to see if someone had been sleeping there. He had left that morning at seven and now it was five. Somebody had definitely had time for a good snooze. Was this a new fad he didn't know about – taking naps in foreign beds before the owners get home? He smelled nothing unusual, but he did find a strange foot-long reddish-brown hair near the pillow on the side of the bed he didn't sleep on. He checked the time on the alarm: 4:00pm. He hadn't had anybody in that bed for months. And the last person, Sarah Fletcher, a student from years before who was now a divorced graduate assistant, had short blonde locks. Somebody had been in his bed and had left before the alarm went off forgetting to turn it to the "off" position. That somebody had long mahogany hair. At least it was most likely a female. But had she bedded down with another somebody who wasn't losing hair? Or who had the cool Charles Barkley shaved head look?

Fuller rubbed under his ear with his left hand and went into the kitchen. Nothing had been touched as far as he could tell. Idem for the living room and bathroom. He went back to the kitchen and poured himself a glass of Chardonnay. He went into the living room and put on Bizet's "The Pearl Fishermen". He finished the wine, lay down and tried to think of who he knew who had hair like the one he found in his bed. He couldn't think of anyone. He fell asleep before the two heroes who are in love with the same woman could sing their famous duet.

The next day at school Fuller began to observe people and their hair more closely. Though it was possible that the person who had borrowed his bed was a complete stranger, the odds favored somebody who knew whose bed they were sleeping in. He was in his office at eight. By eleven-thirty the only person he had seen with long reddish-brown hair was the campus mailman who delivered a stack of anthropological journals to his secretary's desk at ten-thirty. Fuller happened to be walking past his secretary to the rest room when the mail was delivered. The mailman was a male, new on the job, to whom Fuller had never said a word in his life, and who had never said a word to Fuller. But he did have a long reddish-brown ponytail. When he left Fuller asked Sharon, "Sharon, do you know the new mailman"?

"No, why?"

"I found a long reddish-brown hair in my bed yesterday."

"Lucky you."

"We know each other too well."

"What was her name?"

"If I knew I wouldn't be asking about the mailman."

"What's the mailman got to do with it?"

"Didn't you see his hair?"

"No, why?"

"It was long and brown with a red tint."

"Dr. Fuller, if that guy was in your bed yesterday, I'll sign up tomorrow to turn my flesh into McChicken sandwiches."

"Maybe he just came to town and doesn't have a place to stay yet. You know, delivers mail until noon then finds a house with an open door and sacks out for a while in the afternoon."

"There are other people in this town with hair like that."

"I know. You're right."

"You don't remember who you went to bed with?

"That's just it. I didn't go to bed with anyone."

"Oh. So someone borrowed your bed, huh?"

"That's right."

"You sure?"

"No. But I found this hair."

"Was it pretty?"

"As pretty as one hair can be."

"You say it was long, reddish-brown… I'll bet on Julia Roberts."

"I don't even like Julia Roberts."

"I know. You've told me. Too much mouth. Too many teeth. I'd say start examining your students. That sounds like something one of them would do. Watch who comes up to your desk."

"Nobody does. Hardly anybody anyway."

"It only takes one."

"True. Thanks Sharon. I'll keep an eye out. By the way, have either of my daughters called?"

"No."

"Just wondering. It's my birthday."

"How could I forget? Maybe that explains the hair. An early birthday present. Happy birthday Lenny."

"Thanks. Can I take you out to lunch on my birthday?"

"You can take me out to lunch on your dog's birthday. How soon?"

"In an hour. I've got a one o'clock class."

"That's right. Eleven-thirty then?"

"You're an angel Sharon. You just haven't grown your wings yet."

"If I had them I'd probably fly away and leave you."

"That's why you don't have them yet."

"They'd better hurry. I retire next year."

"They'd better. Meet you at Tia Rosa's at eleven-thirty. Mexican okay?"

"It's *your* birthday."

"That's right. Don't forget to wear your sexy dress."

"Heil Hitler." She saluted with a flat palm and Fuller went down the corridor to his office to think about the hair and whatever else was clogging his system.

2

Aside from his daughters, ex-wives, and two or three ex-students, Sharon Juppitt was Fuller's favorite human being. She was sixty-four years old, weighed way more than a tenth of a ton, looked to be descended from every shade of homo-neanderthal (as Fuller once said to her when she asked him what to put down on an application form under RACE, "Look Sharon, figure it this way: your mother and father each had two parents who each had two parents who each had two parents...and we're only back to 1850. Try going back about ninety million years - and that's a low number. Good luck on trying to figure out what race you are." "So why do they put RACE on the form?" "Because they're blockheads."

"That's clear enough. So what do I put?" "Try HUMAN. No, screw that. Try 100 YARD DASH TO THE GRAVE." "Okay, boss."), wore blouses that did little to hide her watermelon chest, laughed at almost everything, typed as many words a minute as most people can think, drove a yellow Pontiac that looked to have flat tires on the left side when she was alone in it - and even when she wasn't... ("Why did you choose yellow?" Fuller once asked. "What would you have chosen?" "I don't know." "That's why I chose yellow."), eyes that looked like she'd stolen them from a bulldog, hair that had absorbed so many dyes it didn't know what color it was to begin with, a mind that was as open as they come, ("You're the only person in the universe," Fuller once told her, "to whom I can say and tell everything and anything.") and a white-toothed smile.

"So what are you having?" Fuller asked behind his Tia Rosa pink, yellow, and purple menu.

"It doesn't really matter. And it all tastes the same. Like hot sauce."

"Have a bowl of hot sauce then."

"The Enchilada Combo plate."

"Yeah, me too."

"Thought anymore about that hair?"

"Absolutely. I like it. I'm saving it. It's going in my

private museum. And I hope whoever's head it fell off of has a body like you and thinks I'm the sexiest sonofabitch to ever brush his teeth. How do you get yours so white anyway?"

"It's the contrast. Dark skin, white teeth. They're really no whiter than yours. Go get yourself a Tahitian tan and yours'll look just like mine."

"You sure about that?"

"Just look at white next to yellow and white next to black. White looks whiter next to black than it does next to yellow."

"I'll use that in my lecture this afternoon. Come to think of it, why don't you give the lecture Sharon, so I can be off on my birthday?"

"You've got nothing better to do…"

"True."

"Then go pour some more Kool-Aid into those poor kids' brains."

(After Sharon had worked in the Anthropology Department for a few years, Fuller had asked: "So Sharon, who's the finest professor on campus?"

"You are."

"Why's that?"

"Because you're the only one who knows how full of shit he is.")

The Enchilada Combos came. They both went to work with knife and fork producing a minute of silence.

"You're right, after the first couple bites it all tastes the same," said Fuller.

"It took you thirty years to figure that out."

"I'm a snail, darling."

"You know that darling stuff doesn't work on me."

"So you think it was Julia Roberts?"

"Sure of it."

"First Lyle Lovett, then Leonard Fuller."

"Maybe she'd do in a pinch. I could put a bag over her head."

"Then you couldn't stroke her long reddish-brown hair."

"I never really liked long hair on women."

"So what's the rest of your birthday got in store?"

"A one o'clock lecture on Mircea Eliade's 'The Sacred and the Profane', then back home to see if the bed's been borrowed again. Maybe I'll go to a movie tonight. I thought a daughter or two might call."

"What's Eliade got to say? You've never told me."

"That my crap's sacred for me and your crap's sacred for you and that all purple-red-blooded human beings have their sacred crap."

"Who says it's crap?"

"Call it whatever you want to. But if rap music and Tommy Hillfucker jeans aren't crap, I don't know what is."

"Don't be so hard on the kids."

"It's not the kids. It's the idiots who convert the kids to their crap."

"Didn't you used to listen to the Beatles?"

"Sure I did. But at least they wrote songs like 'Nowhere Man' to remind you that you were drowning."

"You ever listen to rap? It reminds kids of worse than that."

"You're right again Sharon. Go teach my class. Do you want any dessert? My daughters didn't call?"

"It's only twelve o'clock."

"If they do, tell them I'll be home at three. Maybe I'll catch my new roommate in the act of snoring."

"I'll have a bowl of vanilla ice cream."

"I'll have chocolate. Waiter."

"Mircea Eliade was a wonderful man. Not enough people listen to what he had to say. He could do a lot for tolerance in the world. I had the pleasure of taking a class from him in Chicago before he retired. What he said was never complicated. He never pontificated. He never tried to be abstruse. He thought anthropology could be understood by anybody bright enough to read a McDonald's menu...

"His most famous work, 'The Sacred and the Profane', makes a point that we all can identify with. He says we all have things that are sacred to us and other things that are profane, that is, that are not sacred. What is sacred for one person can be profane for another and vice versa. What is sacred for one culture is profane for another. We all need our sacred objects, sacred places, sacred people. Without the sacred we are not attached to the earth. Some of you might have seen the Fellini film 'Satyricon'. It took place – if I remember correctly – at the time of the fall of Rome. Nothing was sacred and humans just wandered around aimlessly. Nobody was attached to anything. Rather unimaginable, but Fellini really created such an atmosphere...

"The beauty of Eliade's book is that I'm sure everyone in this room can immediately identify things that are sacred for them and things that are not. For some of you, it might be the label on your jeans. The 'Tommy Whatever-his-name-is' brand might be the only one you'll wear. Or maybe it's Calvin Klein or Reebok or Nike. In any case, those jeans have special meaning to you. Not only the jeans, but how you wear them – low, below your underpants. Maybe your underpants are sacred too. You know something is sacred for you if you wonder where you'd be without it. Without your jeans would your self-image suffer? Would you feel you were a lost sheep? Would you feel less than whole...?

"People can be sacred, places can be sacred. Everybody has places where they feel 'at home'. It might be your room or a chair or a park bench or a car seat or your boyfriend's lap, a pew in a church, or a place you go to watch the sun set. It might be on a baseball diamond or a tennis court. My father used to say he could go anywhere in the world and if he could find a tennis court, he would feel at home. He loved tennis. The lines, nets, balls, and rackets were sacred for him. We could even say the sounds – 40-LOVE, DEUCE, FIFTEEN-THIRTY – were sacred to him. However, if you put him in a football stadium he felt like he was on another planet...

"So what does all this mean? First, that all cultures, and all individuals in those cultures, have their sacred symbols. People's lives get defined through those symbols. Mess with those symbols and you're messing with the heart of men. Think what it can mean when somebody burns the American flag or a wooden cross or when a cemetery gets defaced. But it's not just the American flag or the Christian cross. It's everybody's flag. It's everybody's religious symbol. It's soccer in England, basketball in New York City, ice hockey in Canada, cricket in India. For most of us in this room, they could turn every cricket field in the world into a Hyatt Hotel and we wouldn't care. But the Pakistanis would. The people from India would. Somebody would start burning the hotels...

"Second, it means that to be human is to have a sacred side. Eliade found it everywhere he looked. To understand this is to begin to understand other cultures and other civilizations. Look at what is sacred. Respect it. Don't think only your culture is special...

"Third, man can't survive without sacred objects. In 'Satyricon' Rome falls and it falls quickly. People will give their lives when what is sacred to them is being threatened. Just look at the Middle East today. Look at all religious conflicts. Maybe if politicians understood what Eliade was saying, they would approach conflicts differently. Maybe they'd get to the real reason people tie dynamite around their waists...

"And fourth, I'd suggest Eliade had something to say to Wall Street, Fifth Avenue, and Budweiser beer. Advertising in America today does what? It creates a jingle – "This Bud's for You" – it puts an image in our heads, it creates the sacred out of things that are perhaps inherently profane – like beer, jeans, cars, even water. Can you believe that they import Perrier water from France to drink it in New York City and San Francisco? Anyway, I think Business America took a few hints from Eliade. Make a product sacred, make people think they can't live without it... for a while anyway... until something cooler comes around...

"I suggest you all read Eliade's book. It's on your semester reading list. It's short. And like I said, he didn't complicate things. Next week we'll have a look at Edmund Leach. Any questions?"

No questions.

Fuller is home by two-thirty. The only filament he finds in his bed is a grey unevenly looped pubic strand that is nesting in a sheet wrinkle in the middle of the side where he sleeps.

3

Fuller was napping on the couch again inside the glorious sound of "The Pearl Fishermen" when his daughter Laurie called.

"Hi Dad."

"Who's this?"

"How many people can say 'Hi Dad' to you?"

"Hi Laurie. Sorry, I was asleep."

"At five o'clock in the afternoon. Are you sick?"

"No. Just napping. I've been trying to find out who slept in my bed."

"Somebody slept in your bed you didn't know about?"

"I found a long reddish-brown hair."

"Maybe it was the cleaning lady's."

"Could be, except she doesn't come anymore. She moved back to El Paso, closer to her roots."

"Oh. Happy birthday Dad. I forget how old you are, but I know it's your birthday."

"Thirty-three, plus however old you are. I had you and Carrie at thirty-three. Some of us get crucified at thirty-three, others start a family. You're twenty-six, aren't you. So that makes me about fifty-nine long slow orbits old. It's not my fault."

"So what are you doing for your birthday?"

"What I'm doing now. Napping and talking to you."

"I mean later. Have you got a date or anything?"

"Got any suggestions?"

"What happened to that herbal therapist you were dating?"

"Herbal therapy, that's what happened. She started driving me crazy with all her herbal therapy crap. She thought herbal therapy would cure hemorrhoids. She thought herbal therapy would cure herniated discs. She thought herbal therapy would cure pandemics, car accidents, sexual deviancy, and my unique form of brain disease. She was cute until she opened her mouth."

"You're terrible, Dad."

"I know. I'm terrible. Terribly adorable. So terribly

adorable that probably the only date I can scrounge up for tonight will be wearing a black leather mini-shirt and boots up to her knees, and when the chips are down she'll probably end up being a transvestite."

"Dad... Well, I just wanted to wish you a happy birthday."

"Thanks. How are things with you?"

"Not too bad. Ted didn't get the job at West Texas State."

"He wanted a job at West Texas State? Who would want a job at West Texas State?"

"Dad, the market's tough in his line of work."

"Since when don't we need physicists? Has gravity stopped while I was snoozing?"

"Finding a teaching job isn't what it used to be."

"You're telling me. I only applied eighteen places before somebody bit the worm. So what's he going to do?"

"He might have an in at Knox College in Illinois."

"It's supposed to be a great school."

"Really? ... Good."

"Any kids yet?"

"Not that I know of. We're trying."

"What's wrong with that guy? I'll tell you... He thinks too much about quarks and not enough about fertilizer."

"Dad, it might be me."

"Well I want to be a grandpa as soon as possible. I need something to make me feel old. Something to put me in a first class seat on the geriatric train."

"Listen Dad, I gotta go. I promised Ted I'd help him do the shopping."

"Goodbye Laurie. Say hello to Ted. Thanks for the call."

"Bye Dad."

Fuller hasn't seen this daughter since two Christmases ago, which is fine with everybody. He believes that profound anthropological study proves that children need to cut the umbilical cord as soon as possible and take care of themselves. The longer Mommy and Daddy are in the picture the less the child has a chance to be… to be what? To be free? No. Nobody's free. To be independent? Of course. To be real? What the hell does "real" mean? Everything in the damn universe is real. Maybe real in the sense that you're not just a remake of Mommy and Daddy. Or real in the sense that the sooner you fly the coop the more chance you have of being your own man or your own woman. What does "being your own man" mean? I guess it means doing what you want to do and not what your parents want you to do. What if your parents don't want you to do anything? Or what if what your parents want you to do is good for you? Fuller had tried to give them wings and then let them fly. Dolores wanted them out of the house so she could move in with Arthur Barnes. It seemed to work out reasonably well for their twins. Laurie went to Oregon and Carrie went to Santa Barbara. Both had worked good summer jobs during their school years so Fuller didn't have to break the bank to pay for their educations. Laurie married a physicist and Carrie doesn't seem to be in a hurry to marry anybody. She is teaching kindergarten and has an apartment near the beach. Though they hatched at the same time, they are not look-alikes by any means. Carrie resembles her mother – blonde, blue eyes, nice legs, and Laurie her father – brown eyes and what was originally brown hair (her hair is now dyed black and his is dyed grey), dimpled cheeks and a body that is remarkably average. There had been no real rebellion with either child, no drug problems, no inordinate amounts of time spent in front of the mirror, no high school pregnancies. Neither was the homecoming queen, but both are very pleasant looking. They had no religious upbringing other than Fuller's stories about what people believe all over the world. They got tastes of Buddhism, Hinduism, Christianity,

Judaism, Islam, Shinto, Navajo, shamanism, Unitarianism, Darwinism, Marxism, Nietzschism, Capitalism, Walt Disneyism, and a few glimpses at local African and Polynesian metaphysical inklings. Fuller laid a few samples out on the table and neither girl wanted the whole meal. Dolores didn't care because she was into decorating houses and psychoanalysis.

When Fuller hangs up the phone he puts Bizet's opera back on. He has a shelfful of records that he bought during and shortly after his college years and since he has been living alone they are his principal company. As he puts it, "I have a shit load of great friends and they only talk when I want to listen." He has noticed that he will spend a week or two with one composer, then go on to somebody else for a while. Then he'll start over again. The Eternal Recurrence. It is Bizet's fortnight. "The Pearl Fishermen" is getting the most attention. For some reason "Carmen" makes him sad every time he puts it on. Maybe it's the fact that he's never had the pleasure of knowing her and knows that he probably never will.

The phone rings. It's Dolores. She doesn't call every year on his birthday. He has tried to understand what her motivation is when she does. He has an inkling it has to do with how she is getting on with Arthur Barnes. Or might it be a question of random memory?

"Hello darling."

"Dolores, when are you going to stop calling me darling?"

"When Arthur's in the room."

"Sounds reasonable. Laurie just called. She's still not pregnant."

"I know. She called me, too. When she calls one of us she usually calls the other. She always was such a well-balanced child."

"So where's Arthur?"

"Still at work, I guess. His list of patients hasn't got any shorter with Clinton as president."

"What does Clinton have to do with it?"

"He and Monica have middle-aged men drooling and dreaming all over America."

"I just wish Clinton had opened the can of worms and told it like it is."

"How is it?"

"That he and Hillary probably haven't made any whoopie for a decade and he's the most powerful man in the world and what are such people supposed to do... masturbate in the White House shower every morning?"

"Well, don't forget Hillary."

"I wouldn't dare."

"Yes, you would."

"No, I wouldn't... So how are things with you?

Dolores coughs before answering. She is one of a dying race that still smokes a pack and a half a day and is proud of it. "Could be better."

"Could or couldn't?"

"Could."

"What does that mean."

"Could be better, that's all."

Fuller can tell she wants to talk, so he gives her the chance. "I've often wondered what the real driving force is behind your birthday calls to me. My guess is that it's Arthur. You call when things aren't as rosy as they used to be when you and Arthur were on your honeymoon under the desk in his office."

"What makes you think it's Arthur?"

"What would make me think it's not Arthur? You were always kind of a relationship-oriented woman. In fact, most women are, aren't they?"

"Yes professor."

"I like darling better."

"Of course it's about Arthur, you asshole."

"Hey, I'm only your ex-husband. No need to spit in the phone. And you know I'd never pry into your secret world."

"I know. Okay."

"So what is it?"

"To be honest, he's starting to bore me. Not starting, he is boring me. I never should have moved in with him. I should have kept meeting him under the desk."

"Now, now. Everybody has their ups and downs. You always seemed so happy with him. He seems perfect for you. Where I didn't like to spend hours analyzing our relationship, he makes his living analyzing relationships."

"That's just it. I saw him for five years and now I've lived with him for five more. I thought maybe it's time for me to get off the merry-go-round."

"Thought or think?"

"Think, thought, what's the difference?"

"None I guess. Have you talked about it?"

"With him? No."

"Maybe you should. He's probably used to that sort of thing."

"In other people's lives, but not his own."

"Oh? Are you sure?" Fuller thinks how curious it is that he gets along better with Dolores now than when they were married. That is, now when he talks to her it's almost fun. Before it was like work.

"I don't know. Listen, he should be home any minute now. I better start thinking about his stomach."

"I thought he was the cook."

"Whoever comes home first is the arrangement."

"Makes sense."

"So anyway, happy birthday, Lenny."

"Thanks. If Carrie calls, the world will be perfect."

"Any plans for the night? I know it's not my business."

"I might have a date with Julia Roberts. If that falls through, I'll probably take a bath."

"You always said you didn't like Julia Roberts."

"I know. Things change with time."

"Do they? Bye professor."

Placed here, near the end, Fuller rather likes the sound of the word "professor".

Carrie does make the world perfect. She calls from Santa Barbara while he is fixing dinner. Having no husband or live-in boyfriend, life usually seems less complicated than for Laurie. School is fine. The ocean is warming up. Shorts are back on. She should get a raise at the end of the year. She's got a new bike. Her cat disappeared, but returned last night. No, she hasn't talked to Laurie for a couple weeks. She loves her dad. She wishes him a very happy day.

Before sitting down to eat his spaghetti and

croutoned salad, the birthday boy decides that he'll invite new company to his party. He goes to the turntable and puts Bizet back in his cover. He thumbs through the shelf below. He takes off Stravinsky's coat. And what do you know? Old Igor talks all night about his ex-girlfriend, Petrushka.

4

"Professor, there was somebody here to see you about a half an hour ago."

"Really, who?"

"She said her name was Julia, but she didn't give a last name."

"Go suck on a watermelon, Sharon."

"How was your birthday?"

"Lovely. All three of my ex-roommates called."

"Dolores, too?"

"Yes. She says she's starting to tire of living with her mind doctor. But she's been on that rollercoaster before. I'll give her a couple days to swing back on a high."

"How are your daughters?"

"Fine. How are your kids, Sharon? I haven't asked for a while. Shows what an egotistical asshole I am."

"That never bothered me. Not as much as your snoring."

The beauty of Fuller's relationship with Sharon is that she is as neutral as God and as open as a clear blue sky. There is nothing sexual between them; there is no power ladder; there is no intellectual or spiritual competitiveness; there is no image to keep up; she's a woman so there is no testosterone war; there are no family ties to knot or unknot; there is no pride in the balance; there is no concern about saying the right or wrong thing. Fuller considers Sharon not only his best friend, but maybe his only friend.

"Not bad. The kid that was in jail is out now on good behavior. He's back in Albuquerque with his girlfriend."

"Which one was that?"

"Rufus, the oldest."

"How could one of your kids end up in jail?"

"You're the anthropologist." She scratches the back of her neck with her long pink fingernails. "How did Betty Ford wind up in a rehab clinic? How did I end up working for you and all these other bookworms?"

"I told you Sharon, you should start giving the lectures. I'll type the letters."

"Honey, I was lucky my grandmother kept making me read books and bought me that five-dollar typewriter. I'm glad to be right here where I am. I don't need no room full of college-age kids to make me happy. I still got two at home."

"How are they?"

"One thinks he's Michael Jordan and the other thinks he's... what's that guy's name with all the white hats and long fur coats?... Puffy Daddy... something like that. My son spends every dime he has on clothes, jewelry, and rap music, and any penny he finds in the parking lot he spends on women."

"As long as he's not robbing liquor stores..."

"The problem is, the rap stars don't need to rob the liquor stores, but kids like my son do so they can wear the white hats and fur coats, drive the shiny cars, catch the fast women... make that shiny women and fast cars. I don't hear any politicians talking about that."

"If you don't want to start teaching my courses, Sharon, you should at least run for Congress. I'll be your campaign manager."

"You're too nice to me, Mr. Fuller. You know, I should have brought my son in here to talk to you when he got out of the clink. Maybe you could have given him a few tips on how to stay out of trouble. At least a few tips on how to stay afloat in a world where half his friends end up drowning like old tires in a river."

"It would have been my pleasure. But back to business. Did anyone come in this morning?"

"No. I was just pulling your leg. Did you have fun last night?"

"It was one-on-one with Petrushka."

"You got a new girlfriend, Doc?"

"None of your business, sweetheart." Fuller walked behind her and squeezed the back of her neck as he'd squeeze his own chin. Then he rubbed the top of her shoulders.

"I needed that," she said as he stepped away.

"Who doesn't?" he said. "Thirty years of anthropological research has shown me that human necks, backs, and bodies like to be rubbed. I'll be in my office."

He went down to his office to do nothing. Fuller had fourteen months until he could retire. He'd be finished in June 2000. With the new millennium he could finally shut his mouth. He was at a point in life where he didn't really care if he worked or not. There were pluses and minuses to just about everything, teaching included. Coming to the office gave him an excuse to take a walk. He saw some nice young people every day. He saw his secretary. He didn't mind having a ready-made audience to listen to his garbage even if their pants were hanging from their butts and they had earrings in their belly buttons, eyebrows, and Lord knows where else. African American culture was plowing through the USA. African American culture was plowing into Leave It To Beaver culture and the result was Puffy Daddy and Eminem. A hundred years from now anthropologists will have their hands full sorting through the MTV archives. MTV meets Billy Graham. The result: "Friends." At least sex has finally taken its coat off and sat down to the dinner table.

Fuller sat down in his office chair and stared at his desk. The stack of papers he was supposed to correct hadn't moved. He had a graduate assistant, but he usually did the work himself. He had more time than his assistant who was trying to write a thesis ("Home Alone: Television's Structuring of the After-school Brain in Urban American Pre-Teenagers"), trying to support a wife and child, and teaching a couple classes on the side. Fuller wasn't doing anything except saying what he'd been saying for years. ("Everything's already been said, but since nobody listens, it doesn't hurt to repeat things from time to time." Who said that? He couldn't remember, but he used it at the beginning of each school year.) He had plenty of time to correct papers. He decided a year ago that he wouldn't publish another word about anything until he retired. Not only would he not publish, he wouldn't write. They couldn't fire him at his age for not producing. He had nothing more to say. Too much was being said anyway. He'd let others say it. His last two years would be spent giving his lectures and correcting his students' papers. He stopped going to faculty meetings as well. He was no longer the Department Chairman. Nobody would miss him. In fact they probably preferred not having him there. Most of his colleagues in the Social Sciences knew what he thought: everything they were saying today would be shot to shit a hundred years from now. Not only that, but they'd all be dead and wouldn't even get a chance to see their stuff flushed down the toilet.

Fuller had thought this for the last twenty years, but it hadn't silenced him. He had still written, had still debated through journals, had written a couple of books nobody read, had even sent a few articles to newspapers (the New York Times and Washington Post included), a few of which were published. One, "Christianity and Jesus, Worlds Apart", had even created a mini-scandal and had had some of the local parents and clergy calling for his dismissal from the state university. He had argued that Christianity today had absolutely nothing to do with Jesus. For proof he simply pointed out that a high percentage of Christians judged their religiosity by how much money they made, i.e. the more they made, the more they claimed to be in touch with God. He said this in itself was damning, but that Christianity today was so far from Jesus that most "Christians" weren't even able to turn on the smallest light to see how damned far off they were from the original path. In another Fuller argued that anthropology should be taught beginning in elementary school and continue all through high school. He claimed that the only way kids would stop being MTV-doped up idiots and the only way Americans would stop thinking they were the center of the universe was by showing them from a very small age that their culture and values were but one possibility in a vast multi-colored world. He pointed out that, if nothing else, people who studied anthropology were less jingoistic and that the doors to their minds were at least a crack open. The local press called him unpatriotic to which he responded, "If America wants to lead the world, we have to think of the world first and America second." He got a few tomatoes thrown at his front door.

He finally stopped writing even though he received quite a few favorable comments in private. Besides, he was fifty-nine. There was an age and a time for everything. He wasn't going to change the world. He wasn't even going to change the oil in his car. Because he didn't have one. Without an argument he had let Dolores have the Saab because it was just another thing to worry about. He could walk everywhere he needed to go. He gave her the cell phone, too. He had never used it anyway. He had never thought that pushing all those buttons and looking at a little screen was any fun. Phones were bad enough at home. Who would want one in his pocket?

Fuller pulled the first test from the stack. It had the name Sarah Dawson written in the right-hand corner. The writing was very slanted right and Fuller wondered if maybe Sarah had back problems or was in a hurry to go somewhere. He read: *Anthropology differs from Sociology in that Anthropology is about man and Sociology is about society. Anthropology's first concern is "anthro" and Sociology's first concern is "socio".* He didn't read anymore and wrote "Brilliant" and "A+" at the top of the page.

The next paper was by Tony Flowers. It began: *Anthropology and Sociology are pretty much the same because Durkheim was really a sociologist, but we read him in Anthropology class because what he had to say is applicable to Anthropology because society is made up of men and women just like any culture in the world.* Fuller stopped there and wrote "Excellent" and "A+" next to Tony's name.

He picked up one more. Jake McFarland. If he remembered correctly McFarland was a middle linebacker on the football team. An assistant coach had asked Fuller how he thought Jake would do in his class. Fuller had said he'd love to have him. Jake's answer to the question (How does the study of Anthropology differ the study of Sociology? Use concrete examples to justify your answer) began like this: *I took a class last year in Socialogy an the teatcher was a woman who most a the time just showd us a lotta graffs and stuff, and this year in Athropology the teatcher is a lot diferent and mosly talks and tells storys about Africa and the Indians and places like that. I like Athropology bedder so far.* Fuller wrote, "The first seven words are a perfect spiral. Keep working, Jake. Good Luck on Saturday. B+."

Other than McFarland everybody got an A+. He had finished the stack in twenty minutes. Unlike most teachers Fuller thought that the only value of a test was the preparation the students did for the test. The test itself was merely a regurgitation of whatever work the students did or didn't do. The longer he taught, the more he was convinced that the tests themselves were useless. When he thought back to his own career as a student, the only thing he remembered was staying up all night and preparing. He had no memory of the actual tests. The dean of social sciences called him into his office a couple years ago to complain about Fuller's grading. Fuller responded that the problem wasn't his grading, but the idiots that the admission's office let on campus. He said his only concern was teaching something and giving the students a positive image of themselves. He said test results had nothing to do with learning and everything to do with the images the students had of themselves. When the dean countered with, "But when ninety-five per cent of the students have A+es the grade becomes worthless." "Precisely," Fuller responded. The dean decided that since Fuller would be retired in three more years, he would avoid a major fight and sent him out the door.

Fuller didn't tell the dean that all the A+es helped get students to study anthropology who otherwise would never have set foot in one of his classes. He was convinced that the study of comparative cultures could only be a plus in a kid's life, especially a kid who lived in a place as big, blubbery, and near-sighted as America. It wasn't that Fuller didn't like America. He liked it as much as any place else he'd ever been to. It was just that his experience told him a human life was richer when it was able to put itself into a historical, geographical, and cultural perspective. The study of anthropology, even on a bad day, was able to do that.

Fuller pushed the pile of papers back to the corner of his desk. He put his left elbow on the desk and the hand of the same arm slid under his chin. He noticed he hadn't shaved for a few days. This was not unusual because he hated shaving as much as he hated... as much as he hated what? He tried to think of what he hated other than shaving. The only things he could come up with in a few seconds were violence, suffering, and death. Other than that, he didn't hate much. Not even the dean. Not even fast food. Not even MTV. Not even right-wing Republicans or television preachers. He really didn't hate shaving either. It was just a nuisance. Like wiping after defecating. Or a piece of an apple stuck between two teeth. Or ice on the windshield when he'd had a car. Or TV evangelists. Shaving was a nuisance, but having a beard was more of one. He had tried growing one on numerous occasions. That is, he had tried to quit shaving. But every time the six- or seven-day growth produced an annoying itch that brought the razor and foam off the bathroom shelf. His hand stroked the hair. Within a day or two he knew he'd slice it.

His door, already a crack open, squeaked. A pig-pink hand and a blonde head appeared. It was Sarah Fletcher, the graduate assistant who had last helped by releasing the pressure in his aging nuts. "Is the anthropologist in?" she said as her face, round as a pie, appeared.

"He's as in as a nose hair," Fuller said.

"Mind if I join the romantic wonder?" she said pushing the door open and holding out a bottle of wine. "Happy birthday, Leonard. I couldn't come yesterday. I had to go see my mother."

"Today is as good as yesterday. Thanks Sarah. No matter how old or insane I am, I still appreciate somebody remembering my birthday."

"It's universal, professor."

"Really? I'll have to go to the library and do some research." Fuller rises to meet the oily-lipped kiss that is coming his way. Sarah finds his mouth with his help. She releases her hand from the back of his head and retreats to the only other chair in the office.

"How are things?" she asks bending forward and pulling up a sock on her comely ankle.

"Couldn't be peachier. I just finished correcting my tests for the week and somebody, other than you, has been in my bed."

"You don't *correct* tests, Lenny, and what kind of

thing is that to say to someone who brings you a bottle of Idaho's finest Burgundy?"

"A nice thing. I don't know who it was. I wasn't there. You're the last real person I know of to crawl under my sheets."

"What are you talking about, Leonard?"

"Things. How things are. You asked me how things are and I'm telling you about the things that are at the apex of my brain and are struggling down to the tip of my tongue. Another stack of A+es and a reddish-brown hair I found in my bed a couple days ago."

"Whose was it, darling?"

"That's just it. I don't know. I found it in my bed one day after I came home from school."

"You look in your bed for hairs every day after school?"

"I was taking a nap. I found it by accident. Sarah, for once I've got a little mystery in my life."

"The Mystery of the Red Hair. Sounds about as exciting as researching vacuum cleaner bags."

"Reddish-brown."

"Come on, Lenny. How was your birthday? I had to go to Denver, otherwise I would have brought you a cake with fifty-nine flaming red candles."

"Is your mother having problems?"

"Had problems. They took out her uterus last week."

"Ouch."

"I'll tell her you said so."

Fuller looks at the bottle and though it is only nine o'clock in the morning, proposes they sample it.

"You know if I drink a glass of wine in your presence, I become a nymphomaniac," she says. "Especially in the morning."

"I had forgotten."

"Why don't I come over this evening? I'll make you some Thai food."

"Fun we do one bang ding."

"What?"

"I said 'That would be wonderful' in Thai."

"God bless Lenny Fuller. I gotta go," she says heading for the door. "How's about six thirty?"

"Sarah, you're welcome any time as long as we do one bang ding."

"Go read a Margaret Mead book." She blew a backwards kiss as she left the anthropologist's office.

5

Sometimes Fuller longed for romance, but he knew no one wanted to eat a fifty-nine-year-old body. His theory of love was simple: if you love somebody, you want to eat the person. Of course he didn't mean it literally, that is, not in a cannibalistic sense. But if you love somebody, everything about their body is appetizing. He knew his body was no longer appetizing. Maybe his mind was appetizing to someone like Sarah Fletcher, but his body, he was certain, couldn't stand up to other bodies she could find on the market. He was old meat; the expiration date on his label had expired; there were lots of other fresh T-Bones on the racks. Since his second wife, he had had to make do with women who were kind enough to lend a hand in helping him release the pressure in that hanging sack of hazelnuts. He was appreciative, but he knew love was a thing of the past. Love of him, anyway. Yes, he could still love, he could still find women he would want to douse with salad dressing or olive oil and lick every corner of. But he knew it would never be reciprocal. Not anymore.

Sarah was in the kitchen. He was sprawled across his thirty-year-old Sears sofa listening to Stravinsky. The couch fit his body like an old shoe. On the coffee table next to him was one bowl of carrot sticks and another bowl of curry dip. He sipped a glass of French rosé. He wondered if that was why Hemingway had blown his brains out... because his sixty-one-year-old body had slid completely off the menu. He set the glass on the table and stuck another curried carrot between his lips. Of course there were other things to live for, things other than women wanting to eat your body. But not many, not many he could think of. Music sometimes. But music was much better if it was either a prefix or suffix to lovemaking. Ditto for food. Fuller reached for his glass and balanced it on his chest with the help of a finger. Stravinsky's Dance of the Wet Nurses flooded him. How did they get wet? Rain? Gizz? Bobbing for apples? Falling in a swimming pool? Squirting blood?

"Soup's on, birthday boy." Sarah was behind him with some fingers on the side of his face. They smelled like coconut milk. He arched back his head and looked at her. She reminded him of a jelly donut. Not that she was fat. She wasn't really. But like a jelly donut she was rounded on all the edges. There were no edges. She smiled and kissed his forehead. The forehead kiss, he thought before rising from the sofa, was another thing that became more frequent with age. As the teeth twisted, lost fillings, fell out, browned, or just plain rotted with time, who in their sober mind would want to get close to them? French kisses couldn't even be paid for. Lips were avoided unless the passion really hit fifth gear, which was about as often as Hillary Clinton put on a miniskirt.

"Smells delicious," Fuller said. "You've mastered Thai cooking in the time it takes most people to learn to make pancakes. From a mix. Just add water. When did you buy that cookbook?"

"A month ago."

"Well, the last time you made it it was wonderful. This smells even better."

"Flattery will get you everywhere, Fuller."

"Where do I want to go?"

"To bed. To jail. To the Super Bowl. To the White

House."

"I accept A, fear B, couldn't stand C, and D would be fine under the circumstances that Clinton was impeached for."

"I thought you liked football."

"I did, until they started having pre-game shows and half times that last longer than the game itself."

"Advertising darling. What is it now for the Super Bowl, a million dollars a second?"

"A minute."

"Well in a few years it will be a million a second. Don't be so hard on advertising. TV has to make a hard buck just like everybody else. So do those poor football players. They die young. They deserve to be well paid."

"Where was your moral intuition when the gladiators were playing?"

"I was still wearing diapers. You know, Lenny, the longer I live the more I appreciate advertising. How would anybody know what to buy without advertising?"

"Good point, Sarah. But just not at the Super Bowl. It's impossible to stay awake through a four-hour game."

"What about cricket? It takes all day."

"They take naps."

"Then take a nap."

"I do. And when I wake up I don't care who wins

anymore."

"Poor Leonard. But seriously, think about the value of advertising. The brain has its work done for it. It doesn't have to think. It doesn't have to examine all the alternatives before deciding on a purchase. All buying decisions are made for it by advertisers so it is free to use itself to think about important things."

"So true. Like what?"

"I don't know. Like when to vacuum the living room or whether to open your birthday present before or after dinner."

"I love you, Sarah. You already gave me a birthday present."

"I love you too, Fuller. It was love at first A+."

"I wasn't giving A+es then."

"Yes you were."

"I'm losing track of time. For me it was love at first lick."

"You're so romantic. So do you want it now or later?"

"That depends on what it is. Can we eat it?"

"Something's burning."

"My hazelnuts."

"Your what?" Sarah says as she runs into the kitchen.

Fuller sits down at the table and lights the low candles that Sarah has placed around a small bouquet of pink roses. "Do want me to call the fire department?" he calls.

"No, it was only one nem," she calls back.

"What's a nem?"

"That's Thai for spring roll. I thought you spoke Thai..."

"I've forgotten a lot," he mumbles. The kitchen goes silent. He hears a door open and shut. Two minutes later Sarah comes in with a large package shaped like the top of the Capitol Building. She is carrying it like one would a pile of logs, arms out, hands curled back toward the face. It's wrapped in brown paper and red ribbon. She sets it gently on the table. "Be careful when you open it."

Fuller unties the ribbon and peaks down the hole in the top. He sees something moving. He pulls back the paper. He now owns a goldfish and an art deco bowl.

"So we *can* eat it," he says.

"You're terrible. Isn't she cute? I asked the guy in the pet store if fish got bored in a fishbowl. He said not at all. He said they had a memory of four seconds so by the time they swam to one end they had forgotten what it was like at the other end."

"Lucky bastards."

"I got the bowl first. Then I figured you might as well put something in it other than a few bananas. There was a pet store next to the antique shop. I got it in Denver yesterday."

"You brought the fish all the way from Denver?"

"She was in a big plastic bag."

"Why do you keep calling her 'she'? How do you know it's a female?"

"How did I know you were a male? It's intuitive."

"Thanks," Fuller says rising to put a hand on her round butt and his lips on her cheek. "I've never lived with a fish before."

"Me neither. The guy said they're easy to get along with. They don't bark or vomit on the floor. They don't scratch up the furniture. Food's cheap. And with that short memory you can cuss them out when they piss you off and they get over it real quickly."

"Beats a wife. By the way, did you hear the one about the woman driving home in Northern Arizona?"

"No."

"This woman is driving home in Northern Arizona when she sees a Navajo woman hitchhiking. She stops the car and the Navajo woman climbs in. During their small talk, the Navajo glances a few times at a brown bag on the front seat between them. 'If you're wondering what's in the bag,' says the driver, 'it's a bottle of wine I got for my husband.' The Navajo is silent for a while. Then she nods several times and says, 'Good trade.'"

Fuller laughs harder than Sarah.

She goes into the kitchen and comes back with the spring rolls on a plate of lettuce and mint leaves. He fills their glasses with the rosé.

"Santé," he says.

"Happy birthday," she says.

Fuller is happily chewing through Thailand when he feels a large hard chunk of something floating in his mouth. Then he curls his tongue down left. A filling from one of his lower molars has come loose. The dentist had offered him the cheap solution or the expensive solution. He had opted for the cheap solution thinking he might not live long enough to make the expensive solution worthwhile. The dentist had said the cheap solution might last a couple years, but that it could last longer. He fishes for the cheap solution and sets it next to his plate. He is able to keep eating without too much difficulty, but between bites he often sucks air through the corner of his mouth as if he were vacuuming the hole.

"Wonderful meal, Sarah," he says as they get past the chicken curry. "You never told me why you and your husband threw in the towel."

"Just a second. Let me get dessert." She goes to the kitchen and returns with two bowls of fruit salad with a paper umbrella sticking up from each one.

"No birthday cake. Sorry."

"It was yesterday. We're celebrating today. So what happened with you and Romeo?"

"We didn't have kids that's what happened. Having no kids we had no reason to stay together as soon as we realized we weren't made for each other. He was one of these pick-up-every-crumb kind of guys. He started driving me nuts. It was like everything out of place was an invitation to chaos."

"Interesting."

"If something wasn't where he thought it was supposed to be, he would get this look on his face like his world was falling apart. I drove him nuts and he drove me nuts. Fortunately we didn't have a kid or I'd be nuts today."

"Or divorced."

"I probably would have done what you did. Waited til the kid or kids were out of the house. Remember that book by Mary Douglas, 'Purity in Danger', where she talks about how every society has its notion of what is dirt and what isn't. He was at the extreme end of the continuum. Everything was dirt."

"Poor Sarah," Fuller said drinking the juice out of his bowl.

"You're the opposite. Nothing is dirt or dirty."

"Thanks for the compliment." His right hand reached over the table and took her pinkie. His left hand picked up the chunk of fallen filling and dropped it into the fishbowl.

6

Sarah Fletcher is thirty-one years old. She is five foot three and has blonde hair that is chopped around her ears. Her eyes are blue-green, and, like an unpolluted lake in winter, rather transparent. She has round lips, a round nose, round fingers, round forearms, round cheeks, a round waist, round thighs, round calves, and round toes. Surprisingly, only her ankles are rather thin, at least thinner when compared to the rest. Other than these ankles, her whole body is rather the consistency of a baby's butt.

On the night of the Thai dinner, Sarah and Fuller talked more than they usually do before going to bed. Maybe it was the good wine, the company of the goldfish, the length of the meal (four courses, plus dessert). In any case, neither seemed to be in a hurry to take their clothes off. When they finally did, it was Sarah who was first in bed. This, too, was unusual. Normally Fuller drank much more wine than Sarah, tired more quickly, and would be in bed – sometimes asleep – before she had washed, removed what little make-up she was wearing, brushed her teeth, and done whatever else women do before they join Hungry Jack in the bed.

Fuller is drunk, but not that drunk. He has helped Sarah do the dishes and now poured himself a cognac. He sits at the table next to the goldfish. Sarah is down the hall in the bathroom. He is watching the goldfish in the candlelight. First he watches the tail flick, then he wonders why they don't sink or float to the top. They do, he thinks, when they want to or when they die. He watches the path the fish takes, the angles, the turns, the aboutfaces. He wonders about the four-second memory the guy at the pet store talked about. We all only remember what we remember. No matter who we are we don't remember what we have forgotten. Sounds stupid, but it isn't. For some things our memories are less than four seconds; sometimes there is no memory whatsoever. The four-second memory could be a huge advantage when it comes to suffering, but a major disadvantage when it comes to building skyscrapers. But fish are born knowing how to swim. They have a memory that goes back to... back to... back to... just like we do... an instinctual memory... how to suck... how to chew... how to swallow... how to defecate... and then the cultural memory... the symbol... the flag... the word... the Tommy Hilfucker jeans... the star... the cross... the stop sign… the bowed head... blood... the Super Bowl... the Rose Bowl... the fish bowl... values... birth rituals… baptismals... school... mating rituals... death rituals... the collective memory that says this is sacred and that is profane. Is the four-second memory a guarantee against suicide? If you forget everything after four seconds is there never enough time to decide that life is no longer worth living? Does a goldfish ever knowingly, willingly, leap out of its bowl... her bowl... his bowl... to put an end to this swimming, eating, defecating party? For it is a party to which no one is invited but everyone comes. Everyone we know of, that is. Leaving the party is another story. Hemingway wasn't invited but he knew when to leave. With a four-second memory he no doubt would have kept swimming up and down the cool rippled stream. But he remembered what it was like when he had whatever he knew he would never have again. Or maybe he didn't want it anymore. Maybe he no longer wanted what he remembered having and could think of nothing new worth having. Maybe he had pain. Maybe the only new thing was pain and the memory of painlessness was such that pain had to go and the only way of kissing it goodbye was blowing the brains around the riverbank in Ketchum. Lenny Fuller sips the cognac and wonders how long he'll stay at the party. Sarah is under the covers now, warm and round like a muffin not long out of the oven. Does he not love her because he is fifty-nine years old and the only women he can get are women he can't love? But he does love her for her coming and her cooking and her talk and her helping the hazelnut situation. He coughs and the candlelight flickers sending stars to the goldfish bowl. His eyes are locked on the goldfish now as she accelerates in the jumping light. Four seconds later it will all be over. Maybe that's what Hemingway thought. The cognac glass is empty, but not Fuller's memory. He wants to go back to the beginning, to the first moment Leonard Fuller remembers being Leonard Fuller. Was it walking and skirt-tugging between his mother's fine legs while she was puttering at the kitchen sink? Was it playing chess with his grandfather when he was four? Was it lying in his bed looking at the light under the door while he clutched his torn blue blanket? Was it watching his father adjust the camera while he posed in his mother's arms, arms warm like lamps that never let go. Was it …? He doesn't know what it was. Was it a *what* or was it a *when*? Do all whens become whats as soon as the moment passes? Are there no whens? Is temporality one of man's lamer inventions? Is *When I was a kid* always *What I remember about being a kid*?

So what?

He pours another finger of cognac.

While we're at it, he thinks, has anyone ever come within a million miles of describing life?

He blows out the candles and makes his way down the dark hall to the bathroom where Sarah has left the light above the mirror on. As he brushes his teeth his tongue digs in and around the area where the filling fell out. When he rinses, a couple of silver crumbs fall into the sink. He pulls back the left side of his mouth and struggles with the mirror to get a view of the hole. He'll call Dr. Brown tomorrow to care for the crater.

In bed he finds Sarah asleep. He curls up behind her and lays an open hand on the nearest thigh. At five in the morning he is awakened by his steel dong. Sarah rolls toward him and makes her way atop him. And there you have it, the jelly donut and the human drill bit.

7

"So you won't need to tear anything up?"

"Shouldn't have to. We can just do what we did last time. Like I said, it can last a couple years, sometimes a lot more."

"How long did the last one last?"

"What was it? Two years?"

"As long as it outlasts me."

"Let's hope not."

"What's the price difference again?" Fuller squirmed in the chair.

"About a hundred dollars if we do like last time. If we tear it out and build a new one we're talking a thousand or so."

"Last time wins."

"Let's do it then. It'll only take about fifteen minutes."

He didn't even need a Novocain shot. Dr. Brown poked around with one of his silver pickaxes, dried the area, then went to work packing the hole. His nurse handed him a utensil. He pushed, packed, gave it back to her. They did it again. Fuller looked at the light shaped like a hang glider parachute a few feet above his head. He cranked his eyeballs left to get a look at the nurse as she handed the dentist the third portion of whatever it was they were filling the hole with. He could only see her hair. It was reddish brown pulled back tightly around her head. His bed? He hadn't thought about the hair in his bed since his birthday two days ago. Dr. Brown had slipped him in at lunch time between two patients the day after he called. The hair? He tried again to look at the nurse. He saw her neck below her hair. It looked young enough to be his daughter's.

"That should do it," Dr. Brown said. "Now bite down on this." Fuller heard the nurse walk out of the room.

"Is your nurse new?" Fuller said as soon as the dentist removed whatever Fuller had bit down on.

"She's been with me for a month."

"Has she got a place to stay? I mean, is she all settled down here and everything?" The dentist looked at him like he hadn't understood, which of course he hadn't.

"Uh, yeah, I think she lives around the north side of campus. With her boyfriend, last I heard."

"That's where I live."

"Open for me again now. I need to smooth things out."

Fuller tried to say something about the hair in his bed which came out like "UH FON IS E-ISH OW AIR IN I ED E U-ER AY." The dentist politely lifted his head, looked at Fuller, and said, "We've just got another minute or so."

Fuller said, "O-AY," and the dentist again lowered his nose to within a few inches of Fuller's stretched mouth.

When he finally rose from the chair the nurse hadn't returned and the dentist didn't ask him to repeat what he had tried to say. He simply told the patient not to eat for about a half an hour. Fuller thanked him, bit down on his refurbished molar, and said goodbye to the receptionist, a blonde bomber with winged eyelashes.

The dentist's office was south of the campus and not far from his office. He decided to walk towards home instead of going to his office. He had no more classes and was hungry. By time he got home he would have license to chew.

As he walked past the Anthropology building he met Juan José Carlos Rodriguez, his favorite gardener. Juan was bent over a flower bed planting pansies. Fuller tapped him on the shoulder. "Don't get up," he said. "Just wanted to say hello. How's the Garden of Eden?"

"As far as I know, it still beats Juarez," the gardener said looking up then bending away from the glare of the sun.

"Can I buy you lunch? I can't eat for another twenty minutes because I've just been to the dentist."

"Muchas gracias, but I already ate. Had my peanut and jelly sandwich."

"When are you retiring Juan?"

"Probably the same day I die."

"Well, you know I've only got one more year and I'm not sure I'll last that long. Be sure to stop by my office when you've got a minute and we'll go out to lunch."

"Okay, Mr. Fuller. Maybe when you quit I quit."

"How many years have you been here?"

"I start when Kennedy was president. You do the math. When they digging the bullets out of Kennedy's brain, I digging holes for tulips."

"Well, you're the best. Stop by when you can."

It was adios amigos as Juan stuck his hands back into

the dirt. Fuller shuffled off rubbing his tongue on what felt like a mound in his mouth. Amazing, he thought, how in just two days one can get used to something not being there.

He walked west past the main entrance to campus to where the line of fast-food restaurants unrolled like a hose from a fire truck. His half hour was up; he could eat. For whatever reason he felt like a Wienerschnitzel chili-cheese dog. He followed the arrows around the red building to the drive-up window. A young girl with an earring in her nose and another in her eyebrow looked at him standing there. She had on a baseball-style cap and had a microphone in front of her mouth that reminded Fuller of a face mask on a quarterback's football helmet. "This is the drive-up window," she said.

"Is it okay to walk up? I don't have a car."

"You can come in if you want."

"I like it outside. It's a nice day. I've just been to the dentist."

"It's a free country," she said.

"Then let me have one of those large chili-cheese dogs."

"You want onions?"

"I love onions."

"You want extra onions?"

"Extra meaning you don't need them?"

She looked at him like he imagined she would look at a symphony orchestra, "I mean you want extra onions or don't you. Hold on." She talked into her microphone for a minute.

"I'll take extra onions," he said when she finally looked back at him. "And the onions that aren't extra, too." She mumbled into her microphone. Fuller heard her say "sonofabitch" and "fucker". "Drink" came out louder.

"Water would be fine."

"That's two ninety-nine," she huffed.

By the time the money had been exchanged, a hand behind the girl delivered a bag with the chili-cheese dog and a handful of napkins inside. The girl capped a cup of water.

"Thank you very much," he said. The girl ignored the sounds coming from the orchestra and spoke again into the face mask.

Fuller found a bench back next to a small artificial waterfall at the entrance to campus. He wondered how a hot dog could be so different from the person who served it. It was fresh, juicy, and warm. The girl had acted used up, dry, and cold. Fortunately she had been generous with the napkins because the chili-cheese and mustard had painted Fuller's face and hands like a late Pollock. He ate the last bite, drank the water, and wiped the canvas clean. He rose, looked at blue sky nailed to the peaks of the Rocky Mountains, and wandered home like a well-fed camel.

The front door was slightly ajar and he could hear the radio cackling in the bedroom. He didn't wear a watch, but he guessed it was about two-thirty. He tiptoed down the hall listening – and looking – for any sign of human life. He peeked into his sleeping quarters. Since his housekeeper had moved back to El Paso, everything was essentially eternally askew, so nothing had much of a chance to be out of place. The bed was empty. He turned off the radio. It had gone on at two. How had whoever set it known he would stop for a chili-cheese dog? He examined the pillows and sheets. Bingo. With thumb and forefinger he lifted a long dark hair. He held it to the light slanting in through the window; it was a comely shiny reddish brown.

Now he had two. The first one he hadn't really framed, but he had set it on a clean white towel on a lower shelf in the bathroom cupboard. He laid this one next to it. He pulled them tight. They were identical in length and color.

Fuller went into the kitchen and poured a glass of

Chardonnay. He walked to the living room, rubbed the repaired tooth with his tongue, flicked on the turntable and hi-fi, and spread out on the couch. Beethoven had replaced Stravinsky and the Emperor's Concerto was his company. By the time the Second Movement began and the glass had emptied, he had devised his plan: he would ask Juan José Carlos Rodriguez if he had a trustworthy unemployed friend that he could hire to lie under his bed next week when he was out of the house. The intruder would certainly never look under the bed and the hired hand would be able to hear or divine everything that transpired and could get a solid look at the trespasser's feet. Juan's friend would just have to be adept at not making a sound. Fuller resolved to find Juan the next day after his lecture on Edmund Leach.

8

But he didn't talk about Edmund Leach.

"I had intended to talk to you today about Edmund Leach, the famous English anthropologist. Leach wrote a number of interesting books that I suggest you read, like *Genesis as Myth* or *Political Systems of High Burma* or *Social Anthropology*. But as I was walking to campus this morning, I decided to talk about somebody else who, contrary to Leach, is never discussed in academic circles. His name is Juan José Carlos Rodriguez. He is a gardener here on campus. Yesterday he was planting pansies along the walkway outside the building you're sitting in. I decided to talk about him instead of Sir Edmund Leach because he has been more of an influence on my thinking than Leach has. I don't say this to diminish the importance of Leach, but to amplify the life of Juan José Carlos Rodriguez.

"Juan José Carlos Rodriguez was born in Juarez, Mexico about seventy years ago. If you've never been to Juarez, I suggest you go there as part of your education. Juarez and El Paso, Texas are separated by the Rio Grande River, which – at least when I was there – isn't much of a river – at least nothing like you see in the John Wayne movie – but is more like a muddy stream. More than the river separates the two cities, or, if you will, the two countries. There is a lot of barbed wire fencing, too. There are also armed border guards that patrol the area to keep men, women, and children from passing from the south side to the north side. I don't think anybody stops the flow in the other direction.

"Juan Carlos Rodriguez snuck over the border one night when he was younger than all of you are. He had literally nothing except his wet clothes. He certainly didn't have either the English language or any money. He came from a family of seven children who lived in one room in Juarez. His education consisted of trying to find food for himself and his family to eat and learning how to avoid the police when he stole something. At sixteen, he decided to go across the river because on his side he had concluded there was no hope. He came with an older brother whom he hasn't seen since the night they came to America. They had been chased. The brother went one way; he went another. They had agreed that if they got separated they would meet 'at the church at noon the next day' in El Paso thinking that – as in Juarez – there would be one large church in the center of the large town square. It turns out there were four or five churches around the town center and they missed each other. Juan José had been waiting at the Mormon church and his brother Pedro was at the Methodist one.

"Juan José spent that first night hiding under a car that was parked up on Louisville Avenue, which was as far as he had run before running out of breath after crossing the river. Nobody bothered him under the car. When the sun came up he appropriated a clean shirt and a pair of trousers that were hanging on a clothesline behind a house with a low fence. Fortunately it was June and by noon his shoes had dried out, but he had lost his brother. While waiting outside the Mormon church (the building itself was locked) a woman carrying a shopping bag saw him and gave him what amounted to breakfast and lunch: an apple and a donut.

"I'm telling you what Juan José told me. He told me

this more than twenty years ago. I remember it like it was yesterday and, as you can tell, many details have stuck in my mind. I honestly can't say the same thing about what Edmund Leach told me.

"Juan José waited until the sun was angled at about three o'clock and then suddenly thought he had better get away from the scene of the crime, that is from El Paso. He headed west. He made his way out of the city and walked twenty miles across the desert toward Las Cruces, New Mexico. He stayed near enough to the road to where he could see the cars, but far enough away so that no one could see him. He had a moon and a trickle of car lights to give him comfort. He slept in the dirt. He drank from the bottle of water a man had given him at a gas station on the edge of El Paso. The man had understood 'agua, por favor'.

"The next day he walked another twenty miles and arrived in Mesilla, a small town adjacent to Las Cruces, which, according to legend, once lodged Billy The Kid in the local jail. He hadn't eaten for two days and instead of begging or stealing he presented himself at a restaurant that was run by Mexicans. They fed him and hired him to wash dishes. He washed dishes there for fourteen years. It was here that he met his wife Conchita and here that they had two babies.

"To make a long story short, Juan José eventually got into gardening, eventually was given amnesty and a green card, and eventually moved to Colorado after his wife died and his children left home. He told me he had considered going back to Mexico, but a friend convinced him that whatever life he had had there would be gone and that he would be better off staying in America.

"This morning he is outside this building planting flowers.

"I tell you about him for three reasons, none of which you will be tested on. In fact, nothing we talk about today will appear in any evaluation of your intellects.

"The first reason I tell you about Juan José is to get you to respect the campus gardeners, most of whom have similar stories. When I was your age, a gardener was an invisible man. He was 'a gardener' and nothing more. He had no life attached to his gardening. I saw him outside of time like one sees the desk one is sitting at or the hamburger one eats at McDonald's. One does not see or feel the tree that was chopped and the logger that chopped it and the factory workers that cut the wood or the designer who designed the desk and so on. One does not see the cow that was slaughtered to make the meat patty or the tomatoes that were harvested for the ketchup or the wheat that waved in the field to make the flour for the burger bun or the workers who picked the tomatoes or swept the floor in the bun factory. Every person you see and each thing you touch has a history, an infinitely complicated and unfathomable history. No one asked to be born in Juarez, Mexico into dirt poverty. No one *asks* to be born who they are and where they are. Nobody, not queens, not presidents, not ditch diggers, not priests, not prostitutes, not pretzel makers, not professors. Every creature on the face of the earth has his or her own story to tell. I ask you to respect that story. You don't have to agree with it or like it, but at least respect it and understand its complexity.

"The second reason I have told you about Juan José Carlos Rodriguez is so that when you study social sciences you should never forget that you are dealing with real people. Every statistic is made up of real people. Every cultural tradition is practiced by real people. Every belief is believed by real people. Every god that is talked about and every moral notion that is plastered on the planet comes out of the mouth of a human being. Every pair of shoes that are made, every meal that is cooked, every house that is built, every war that is fought, every kiss, every murder, every smile, every fart, every book that is written, every film that is made, every song that is sung, all this comes from people.

"And now, what are people? What is a person? Anthropology is supposed to be the study of man, but what is a man? I ask you to respect man. I ask you to remember that the social sciences are about real human beings. But what are real human beings? Do I know? Do you know? Does a doctor know? Does a physicist know? Does an astronomer know? Does a biologist know? Does a chemist know? Does a priest know? Does the Pope know? Does a policeman know? Does a judge know? Does a psychiatrist know? A university president? A mother? A father? A senator? A terrorist? A drug dealer? A rap singer? An opera singer? Bob Dylan? Jennifer Lopez? Prince? Madonna? Michael Jackson? Michael Jordan? Bill Clinton? Dan Rather? Jay Leno? God? The Devil? The anthropologist? Edmund Leach? Juan José Carlos Rodriguez? Does anybody know what a human being really is?

"My best guess is no. No, nobody really knows what a human being is.

"Why do I guess no? Because if I can teach you one thing, if I can get you to think about one thing, it is to step back and try to get a perspective on everything you believe, every moral value you espouse (including the label on your jeans), everything you consider important and true, every goal you give to yourself and the world.

Ask yourself where your ideas come from. Ask yourself why you believe what you believe. Look around you and what do you see? If you open your eyes you will see a lot of sheep with a lot of different colored fur. You will see American sheep. You will see French sheep. You will see Catholic sheep. You will see Jewish sheep. You will see leftist sheep, right wing sheep, Christian sheep, Islamic sheep, Buddhist sheep, atheistic sheep. You will see herbal healing sheep, sports sheep, cinematographic sheep. You will see journalistic sheep, literary sheep, television sheep, fashion sheep... and *bhhaaa, bhhaaa, bhaaaa.*

"So what does this tell you? What does it tell you about human beings? What does it tell you about ANTHRO-pology? What answers does it give you? Does man have a soul as most religions would have us believe? Is man a materialistic machine, as most scientists would have us believe? Is the truth somewhere in between as many compromisers would have us believe? Or is the truth somewhere way, way, outside? Has this dichotomy got it all wrong? Maybe there is neither soul nor matter. Maybe man is something very other.

"And did man evolve? But evolution implies evolution toward something. Who can prove that man or the world or the universe is evolving toward something? And why is man the measure? Why does man judge everything from HIS point of view?

"Do you know why? Because what the hell else can he do? So when he judges his own knowledge and intelligence it is always he who sets the rules. Maybe this is why he needs gods. To tell him if he is right or wrong. But if they are his gods he is right back where he started from, looking at himself in the mirror and babbling about men being this and men being that.

"So when you walk out the door today look for a gardener. When you find one, you will see a man, a deep man, deeper than you or I will ever know.

"Then look for the sheep, the colorful various sheep. Which color are you? Or are you a horse? Or a wild animal?

"Thank you for attention. See you next week."

9

Two hours later Fuller found Juan José Carlos Rodriguez posing pansies. He didn't tell him he had been the subject of his babble. "Juan, I need you to do me a favor," he said.

"I do for you what I can."

"Do you have any friends who aren't working next week? I need somebody for a few hours every day."

"I'm not working," Juan said. "I have two weeks' vacation and where you want me to go?"

"If you're free, so much the better. I'll pay you fifteen dollars an hour."

"You need trees planted? Grass cut? Flowers? What you need, professor?"

"I need somebody to hide under my bed and see who's napping in it when I'm not there. All you have to do is tell me what you hear and whose feet you see."

Naturally the gardener had no idea what the professor was talking about, but Fuller slowly explained everything about the reddish-brown hairs and the radio. Juan agreed to meet him in his office at ten o'clock on Monday morning. From there they'd go back to his house. The fifteen dollars an hour was more than he was making in gardening. He tried to talk Fuller down, but there was nothing doing. He'd be there at ten.

Fuller had nothing to do so he went to his office and found Sharon Juppitt in a rare state, unhappy.

"Let's go for a walk," he said. "Let the world smile on you."

"Can't. I've got work to do."

"Anything I can do to help? he asked laying a hand on her hefty shoulder.

"Yes, as a matter of fact there is," she said.

"Shoot."

"My son, Rufus, just got kicked out of his girlfriend's apartment in Albuquerque."

"With or without the girlfriend?"

"Without. She threw him out, not the landlords. He wouldn't tell me why. He just said he had no money and no place to stay. When he has no money and no place to stay he usually does something stupid."

"Most people do. So what did you suggest?"

"I told him to come and stay with mama."

"Good suggestion."

"But every time he comes and stays with mama he drives everybody in the house crazy including himself."

"Not so good."

"I just Western Unioned him a hundred bucks for the bus ride up here. He'll probably be here tomorrow."

"Better with mama than in jail."

"He'll probably end up in jail. He usually does one way or another."

Fuller rubbed his nose. "I've got an idea. Remember, you once suggested I, Professor Lenny Fuller, talk to him. So why don't I talk to him? I don't know if I can do anything, but let's give it a try."

"That's exactly what I had in mind. Great minds have met."

"It'll be my pleasure. I've got nothing better to do."

"Yes you do. You got that little ball-a-fire, Sarah, to take care of."

"And the goldfish. She gave me a goldfish for my birthday. Have to change the water every other day. Exhausting work."

"He's gonna call me to tell me when the bus gets in. I'll see if I can convince him to talk to you. No I won't. I'll bring him right here and sit his butt down until you've got time for him."

"Fine with me. I'm free all afternoon tomorrow."

"You're my man."

"You be my woo-man." He kissed his secretary on her ear and went to the toilet, then to his office.

As he sat down, the phone rang.

"Lenny's Laundry. We take spots off leopards..."

"Lenny," Sharon said, "got the dean on the line. He doesn't sound very happy."

"He shouldn't be. Although idiots are known to be happy."

"Lenny..."

"Sharon..."

"I told him you were here."

"Of course you should tell him I'm here. I love talking to him."

"I'll put him through. Don't say anything I wouldn't say."

The phone clicked.

"Doctor Fuller?"

"No, this is Doctor Emptier. Emptier than ever..."

"Dr. Fuller. This is no time for jokes. In the last two

hours I've had complaints from an Islamic student, a Jewish student, and a Christian student about a lecture you gave this morning. I'm surprised I haven't heard from an atheist."

"You should have. I said they were full of it, too."

"Doctor Fuller, I don't know what we need to do. This has got to stop."

"What's got to stop is that we should stop calling this place a university. It's not a university. It's not about higher learning. It's about feeding pabulum. It's about you trying to pacify a community of idiots. Nobody's looking into the universe. Nobody's whacking at the truth. Nobody's really digging."

"Except you, I suppose."

"I didn't say that. I said 'nobody is digging'. Maybe I try to pick up a shovel once in a while. But I don't claim to be getting to China."

"So what do you claim to be doing by insulting religious beliefs?"

"I'm not insulting religious beliefs. I'm insulting all beliefs. All I claim to be doing is getting a kid or two to think for five seconds about who they are, why they believe what they believe, and whether or not that belief is founded on anything other than quicksand and tradition."

"What's wrong with tradition?"

"Nothing. But call it tradition and not truth. I doubt the world would have a war over Halloween. But we tend to cut off a lot of heads in the name of God."

"I think we need to take this up with the president."

"I think that's an excellent idea. I think we should take it up with his wife, too. And his milkman."

"Fuller, you're pushing me..."

"I'm not pushing you. I'm playing telephone with you. I tell you one thing and you'll tell the president another."

"I'm calling the president."

"Call Hillary while you're at it." The phone clicked on the other end. Sharon walked into the office.

"Lenny, you'd better be careful. I was standing outside your door. You were pretty rough on him."

"I know. I shouldn't be. It's not his fault they made him dean. I just wish we could turn the lights on around here once in a while. Maybe I should just quit. What do I care what anybody teaches or what the dean thinks? Or the president? Maybe I should stop."

"Then who would I have lunch with?"

"Your son Rufus."

"Very funny."

"I can't wait to see him."

"Yes you can. He's no piece of chocolate cake."

"Next to the dean he is."

"How do you know?" she said backpedaling. "Listen, I've got to get back to work."

"I've got to get back to looking at the skin on the back of my hands. That's what I was doing when the dean called. It's getting thin and see-through with that purple tint my grandmother's hands used to have."

"That's why some of us stay fat. Keeps the hands young."

"I love you Sharon but get the hell out of my office. I'm getting behind schedule. I need to look at my feet, too."

"See you tomorrow, doctor. My adorable son will be rap, rap, rapping on your door."

Fuller stayed in his office until the sun went down. He looked at his hands, his feet, his arms, and the objects surrounding him in the room that had had his name on its door for thirty years. The wall to his right was a big bookcase with books stacked at all angles, almost none of which he had looked at in the last dozen years. On the opposite wall was a single Navajo rug that he had bought from an old woman in Monument Valley in southeast Utah. He had driven through there the summer before he entered graduate school. The woman was dressed in traditional Navajo garb and was weaving next to a dirt road that tourists used. She was killing two birds with one stone: she'd weave and when a tourist stopped she'd ask for a dollar to lend her authentic self to the foreground of a picture of the baked rust-red towers. Fuller had taken both birds: he paid the dollar and fifty more for the rug. He had never forgotten the woman. She, in all likelihood, had forgotten him. That's the way life works, he thought. But every time he looked at that rug he saw her face framed in the cobalt-blue sky with a couple of billowing clouds hanging left and right to balance the photograph.

He kissed the rug and walked across campus in the twilight. At home he found nothing in his bed and the radio was as quiet as the dead. He fed his goldfish, heated a frozen pizza, ate it in the gentle rain of the second movement of Beethoven's Violin Concerto, and was asleep on the couch before both the turntable and the world stopped spinning.

10

"Hey, nice to meet you, Rufus," the professor said. "I've heard a lot about you from your mother.

"Shit, no doubt."

"Some, no doubt, but not only." The professor was trying from the word go to find a meeting ground of mutual confidence. He started with the two words, *no doubt.*

"I'm tired, so I hope this don't take long."

"I'm tired, too."

"You ain't been on no fuckin' bus for two weeks."

"How long was the trip from Albuquerque? That's where you came from, wasn't it?"

"I don't know. I left last night at eleven."

"Well thanks for stopping by."

"Why you thankin' me?"

"I guess because, other than your mother, I don't get many visitors these days."

"You want visitors?"

"Depends on my mood."

"Don't it for everybody. There was even times in the clink I didn't want no visitors."

The professor decided to avoid the subject of prison. The young man across from him was slouching further in the chair with each minute. He was wearing the baggiest jeans Fuller had ever seen that were now piled at his feet. When he walked in the door, Fuller had noticed he had beige boots on. He was sporting a white T-shirt referred to in common jargon as "a wife beater", and over that he had a burgundy and black leathery jacket. He had a large silver chain and cross marooning on his chest, a tattoo crawling up his neck, earrings in both ears, and a black silky cloth glued to his head. A set of headphones, from which a chord ran to a jacket pocket, dangled below his ears. His skin, Fuller thought while wondering down what road to pull the conversation, was the color of his living room table, to wit, a pleasant deep mahogany, rather like Guinness beer. He looked at his own pinkish-green hands and tried to imagine what color label Rufus would give his face.

"So Sharon said you got booted out of your apartment?" Fuller said hoping the use of the mother's first name was appropriate.

"I ain't have no use fo the bitch anyways."

"My first wife didn't have no use for me. But she didn't throw me out. She *outed* and left me with the mortgage and moved in rent-free with her boyfriend."

"How many wives you had?"

"Two. The second one died."

"Sorry bout that." These three words, and the way they came out, made Fuller believe that Rufus Juppitt had enough of his mother in him to make it through this world, one way or another.

"She hit a tree. The car died, too. Both totaled. Skidded on some ice." He decided to shorten a few sentences to try to catch the linguistic wave that he imagined carried Rufus and his peers.

"Friend a mine hit a fuckin' telephone pole. He didn't come out no better. She on crack?"

"Not that I know of."

"My friend was."

"Cars are dangerous. People usually figure this out too late, crack or no crack."

Rufus went silent for a few seconds, played with his lips, scratched his unshaven face (here was one thing they had in common), then said, "What you teach anyway?"

"Anthropology. The study of man."

"No shit. Lot a assholes out there for studyin'."

"You're telling me."

"So what kind a shit you teach?"

"All kinds. Over the years I've tried to dilute the shit to a minimum such that it comes out in a more edible fashion." Fuller hoped his re-use of the word *shit* would have the desired effect.

Rufus looked at the shelves of books across the room.

"You mus read a lot."

"I used to, but I don't anymore."

"Me neitha," Rufus said rolling his eyes ceilingward and chuckling.

Fuller thought the moment was as good as any to get to where he wanted to go. He hoped the oven was warm enough such that the cake wouldn't sink right away. "So I teach a lot about different cultures around the world and try to help the students get a feeling for why people are the way they are and why one group of people acts one way and another acts in a very different way." Rufus didn't say anything. Fuller kept going. "Among other things, I try to get students to understand that every human being is born into a cultural setting that colors who he or she is and what he or she thinks and how he or she acts. If you move around the world, it's pretty obvious that people tend to have little choice about who they are."

"What do you mean?"

"I mean an Eskimo tends to be like other Eskimos, an Indian tends to be like other Indians, a kid from Harlem tends to be like other kids from Harlem, a kid from the rich suburbs tends to be like other kids from the rich suburbs. I try to get students to realize that culture is a very powerful thing, but if *they* are powerful, they can step back a little and instead of just following the crowd, can try to decide to be what kind of person they want to be and not just be a sheep in a herd."

Rufus wiggled in his chair. "You really teach that shit in college?"

"I try to. I don't know how good a job I do, but I try to. When I was about your age, I started asking myself how much of what I was was the result of my white, middle class, Christian American upbringing. I tried to figure out if I was just a function of my culture or if I was my own man."

"You tryin' to tell me I ain't my own man?"

"Not yet. I'm trying to tell you that I found out that

I wasn't *my* own man. You can tell me later about yourself. You can tell me now if you want to." Rufus fiddled with the headphones around his neck, then he stood up and took off his jacket.

"It hot in here." With only his wife beater covering his upper body, Fuller saw a tattoo exhibition on his thick muscular arms. He had heard that prisoners spend a lot of time doing pushups and lifting weights. "So what you getting' at?" Rufus said as he sunk back to sea level.

"You tell me."

"You tryin' to tell me we all dumb fucks."

"Partially. But I'm also trying to tell you there's hope, there's hope of being less a dumb fuck than some of the other dumb fucks. I'm telling you the same thing I'd tell the Pope or the President of the United States. I'm telling you to dig down, see what your roots look like, appreciate other people's roots, then choose what *you* think is right and not what your culture tells you is right."

"What you mean, 'right'? If I ain't doin's what the cops 'n the judge think is right, they put me back in the fuckin' can."

"Point well taken. But I mean that if you have, let's say about seventy years to spend on this earth, are you going to spend them dog paddling around in the swimming pool of your culture or are you going to climb up on the high dive, look down, and invent your own life?"

"Who says you gots seventy year? Where I come from, it more like twenty-five."

"Well, the number of years isn't necessarily what we're talking about. It's how you use the ones you've got."

Rufus rises and walks over to the bookshelf. He picks up a book, flips through it, then puts it back where it was. "You mus think youz pretty fuckin' smart."

"Not really. I know and fear my limits. But I think I'm smart enough to know how small most of us really are. I'm also smart enough to know it isn't necessarily a good thing for a small person to become big. Most people can't handle being bigger. There aren't many leaders out there, but there are a whole lot of followers. But right now, I'm really just thinking about you and me."

"So wha you think bout me?"

"I don't know. Too early to tell. But I've got an idea, Rufus. For both of us. You and me. To see if we can climb up on that high dive. It's something I've always wanted to do, but never have. I want us to exchange clothes. You walk out the door wearing what I've got on and I walk out wearing what you've got on. We keep our underpants and socks, of course. But everything else we exchange." Rufus looks at Fuller and chuckles, "You one crazy muthafucker."

"Our clothes are a function of our culture, right? You wear what you wear because it's cool to look that way. I wear what I wear because I think I'm cool. My culture, your culture. Let's switch and see what it feels like. You walk out dressed like the professor, and I walk out dressed like the... the what?"

"The bad muthafucker."

"Okay, the bad motherfucker. And if I'm not mistaken, the bad motherfucker look is the look of most of the rap music singers."

"You ain't mistaken. But you is mistaken cause I ain't gonna do it. My partners'd kill me."

"But you haven't lived around here for a long time. Aren't most of your partners a thousand miles away? And I'm only talking about one day. We change for one here-today-gone-tomorrow little day."

"Be a helluva long little day."

"Not necessarily. It might be fun. Might be a short day."

Rufus thought for a moment, exhaled audibly, wiggled his head, ran his shiny pink tongue around his mouth, poked it past his teeth and said, "Fuck it. Why not? You the one people know round here. I'd be a pussy ta say no."

"If you say yes, you're no pussy. I'm the pussy. I'm fifty-fucking-nine years old. I've been an anthropology teacher for thirty years. I'm a year from retirement, if I don't get fired first. I've wanted to do this for years. But I've never changed clothes with anybody. You're perfect. We're perfect. We're on opposite ends of the great American spectrum. Actually, maybe we're not. Maybe we'll find out."

"So one day and that's it..."

"Twenty-four hours. We change, walk out the door, and meet back here at four o'clock tomorrow afternoon."

"Awright. Fuggit. You on, Jack." Rufus smiled a herculean smile. "My mutha said you was one crazy muthafucker."

They began to peel off their clothes. Fortunately, they were about the same height. Fuller's corduroy pleated olive-green pants and old beat-up penny loafers fit Rufus fine. His poorly ironed Ivy League shirt was a tad tight in the armpits. His round-neck black wool sweater fit Rufus's torso like a wet suit, like Jay Leno's sidekick musician wears his. Rufus showed Fuller how to keep the pants low on the butt without them falling. There was a wide belt to help. The wife beater allowed the garden of grey hairs on his sagging chest to be seen. Rufus attached the black "do-rag" affair to Fuller's cranium. The boots, untied, were fine. Lastly Rufus took his weighty chain and cross off and fastened it around Fuller's skinny neck.

"I hope you ain't got no date tonight, professa."

"I'll try to get one," Fuller said.

"So what the rules?"

"No rules. We just have to wear the stuff until tomorrow except when sleeping. Let's go say hello to your mom." Fuller put on the bulky blood and black jacket and set the headphones around his neck.

"You gotz sunglasses in the other pocket," Rufus said. "You gonna need 'em." Fuller put them on and out the door they went.

"You're a helluva guy, Rufus," Fuller said glancing behind him as they sauntered down the hall.

"Fuck you," Rufus murmured.

"Oh my Lord!" Sharon Juppitt cried.

11

As he walked across campus, Fuller started dipping his shoulders, first right, then left. He knew there was a strut that went with the look and he tried to find it. *Right foot, right shoulder. Left foot, left shoulder.* He stopped and turned on the Sony machine in the jacket pocket. He put on the headphones and then mercifully turned down the volume. But walkways and the Rocky Mountains were alive with the sound of music.

> *They say the bitch is rich, ain't found her niche*
> *Fuckin all day and all night*
> *She don't even care if they turn on the light*

Fuller cringed and turned off the music. No wonder Rufus's girlfriend had thrown him out.

He never wore dark glasses, but now realized why people did. You can look at whomever you want without them knowing who you're looking at. The head can keep straight, but the eyes can wander. There was a certain feeling of playing god or the voyeur: I can see you but you can't see me. People looked at him, but few manifest anything other than a quick second glance after they had passed. A male student said to the girl at his side, "Check out Eminem's grandpa." A Britney Spears clone said, "Hey, haven't I seen you on MTV?" Otherwise he got across campus unmolested.

The pants were set far below the waistband of his boxer shorts, but miraculously they stayed up. Rufus had tightened the belt to a maximum. The untied boots felt a size too big. Fuller wondered how Rufus was doing in his loafers.

He needed a few things at the grocery store, so before going home he went to the Safeway supermarket. As he walked through the parking lot, a man in a red pickup truck wearing a cowboy hat and a plaid shirt pulled up next to him and stared. The window descended and the man said, "You guys having a fuckin' Halloween party back at the old folks' home? Can I give you a ride back?"

Fuller removed the sunglasses and smiled. "As a matter of fact, I thought you might want to join us. Your outfit is as good as mine."

"Go build yourself a coffin," the man said as the window went up and a screeching of tires accompanied his departure.

In the store things were different. An old woman weighing a sack of apples grinned at him and said, "I like your style. I thought about gettin' me some of those big jeans. They look as comfy as comfy gets."

"They are. No crotch rash with these babies," Fuller said.

"You always dress like this or are you an actor or something?"

"Just doing my shopping."

"Well, it is a free country. Maybe we need more

people like you to narrow the generation gap.”

“I don’t think it’s just a generation gap,” Fuller said. “I’m afraid there are a lot more holes than that in this nice little society.”

“You European or something?”

“No, home spun American just like you.”

“My ancestors come from Scotland.”

“Mine too. Small world.”

“Well, I’d better be moving along before my husband gets worried. He gets worried if I take too long in the toilet. Forty-nine years of worrying. You’d think he stop by now. Won’t stop till they cover him with dirt.”

“It was nice talking to you.”

“You too.”

A chunky boy of about fifteen with a blond crew cut came up and said, “Hey man, my name’s Poncho. I like your threads. Where’d you get those jeans?”

“Actually a friend lent them to me.”

“They’re cool.”

“Thanks.” Fuller thought that this had to be the first time in years that a boy that age had spontaneously talked to him. “My name’s Lenny,” he said.

“Nice to meet you Lenny.”

As Fuller was getting a packet of coffee, a man in his twenties stocking shelves looked him over and said,

"Wish my old man dressed like you. You like rap music or something?"

"Not really," Fuller said. "I'm more into classical."

"You'd never know it by looking at you."

"Well, different strokes for different folks, I guess," Fuller said.

"Can I help you find anything?"

"No thanks, I'm fine." Fuller thought how many amazingly friendly people there were in America. Sure you had your assholes, but overall the country was a happy place. He remembered coming back from Europe a few years ago and, aside from the people at the airport passport control, noticing how his fellow citizens were such amiable souls.

He walks the rest of the way home in relative anonymity. Sarah's Ford Fiesta is parked in his driveway. "It's me," she yells hearing the door open.

"Was the radio on when you got here?" he shouts back taking off the coat in the entrance hall.

"No. Why?"

"Just wondering. The hairs in the bed have a tendency to leave the radio on."

"What?"

"Just checking up on who's been to the hotel."

"Do you still think somebody's been sleeping in your

bed?"

"I know so. Just like I know God created the world, put it in the oven, then forgot about it." He tromps into the kitchen almost forgetting he has his outfit on.

Sarah glances up, "You been shopping?"

"Safeway's."

"No, I mean the getup."

"No, I just changed religions. Converted to Eminemism. Actually I traded clothes with Sharon's son. We're doing a little experiment."

"You're cute. I once had a boyfriend who dressed like that. He was actually a nice guy. Looked like Al Pacino."

"Well, I once had a girlfriend who dressed like you. Her clothes were so ugly, all I ever wanted to do was take them off."

"Very funny. Are you hungry?"

"What's cooking?"

"Lasagna. And I bought a bottle of Chianti. It'll be ready in half an hour."

"A slave must eat."

"Really, what's with the clothes?"

"I'm seeing if I can get Rufus Juppitt to realize that his gangster – or whatever it is that knocks him into jail – lifestyle might not be the only road available to him. At the same time, I'm seeing if being a teacher isn't the only road open for me."

"You're a little late if want to start hip-hopping. When was the last time you saw a fifty-nine-year-old duck turn into a rabbit."

"He's a great kid, I think. I couldn't believe he went for the idea..."

Rufus Juppitt went home with his mother at five o'clock. She lives on the southeast side of town, the part of the city farthest from the mountains and closest to the highway and railroad tracks. Her husband left when Rufus was five and the youngest was two. She didn't really mind because she didn't love him. She didn't try to bring him back. A family without a father was nothing out of the ordinary for her; it was as normal as the golden arches at the entrance to a McDonald's restaurant. She had a job; the kids ran free; they would lead the life that a borderline ghetto habitat served up. Rufus, like his brother, robbed and peddled drugs. He had been caught, his brother hadn't.

"I ain't that stupid, Mom," he said in the car on the way home. "Your teacher friend ain't tellin' me nuthin' I don' awready know. That's why I done it."

"He just doin' me a favor. He's the only man I know who I thought might have something to say to you. So why'd your girlfriend throw you out?"

"Same ol' shit. She thought I be screwin' another bitch."

"Were you?"

"Course I was."

"Why?"

"Why we all do? Feels good. Makes us feel like weez king uh the fuckin' heap. Why does Jordan score forty, then when the game be ova he gotta go out and score some more?"

Sharon didn't say anything. She pulled into a gas station not far from their house. Rufus asked her if she wanted to fill it up. She stared through the windshield and nodded. She reached into her purse and gave him twenty dollars. He got out, pre-paid the gas, and started to fill the tank. As he stood there squeezing the nozzle, a Boyz 'n the Hood crew pulled up next to them in a fire-engine red Lincoln Continental. The music was blasting into the world, the shades shading out the world. A guy in the back seat got out, looked at Sharon, then Rufus, and said to Rufus, "Hey pitbull, where your master?"

Rufus ignored him, capped the tank, and got back into the car.

"Let's go out to dinner," Sharon said. "On the other side of town. How about the Sizzler?"

"Fucker," her son said half smiling, half looking hard at nothing and grinding his teeth. "Yeah, I ain't eat shit all day."

Sharon looked at him like at a naked baby. Her baby. The momma don't stop lovin' her baby. "I guess the professor knew what he was doin'. I wonder what kinda treatment he be gettin'."

"Me, too." He bit his lip. He didn't have a gun so he couldn't shoot anybody. People got shot for less.

Sharon made a U-turn and got on the freeway going the other way. Dinner in the Sizzler went with no incident. Parts of America were finding a middle ground, a demilitarized zone where the milk was homogenized and left a little room for dissonance on the edges.

When they got home Rufus's two brothers were on the couch watching a Nuggets-Lakers game. They looked at their brother as if they were wearing thick glasses. "They give ya the wrong bag when ya got outta prison?" the younger one – the ball player – said. He got up and and gave his brother the beautiful handshake and hug routine. The other brother then said, "You rob the Salvation Army or summin'?" and got up and greeted Rufus. Rufus bit on his tongue and was holding back tears. He hadn't expected any special emotion, but the scene – the world – his world – was getting to him. Even the hardest bodies have cotton corners.

He sat down in the armchair to the left of the sofa, ran his hand through his short, matted hair, and looked around the room that he hadn't been in for three years. "You guys look good," he said.

"Can't say the same bout you," the gangsta brother said jokingly.

"Three hours ago I looks like you," Rufus said.

"What happened?"

"Momma's boss got aholda me."

"He steal yo shit?"

"No, we exchanged clothes. An expirment. Ta see what it feel like to dress like the utha guy."

"He just want yo shit, man," the gangsta said.

"He fitty-nine-years-old," Rufus said. "He don' want my shit. Momma want him to lead me outta da shit to da promised land."

"Where that?"

"Outta jail," Sharon said from the adjoining kitchen.

"He awready outta jail," the gangsta said.

"We're talkin' about not goin' back. We're talkin' about maybe doing something in life other than messin' people's lives up including our own," Sharon said.

"What for dinner?" the gangsta said.

"Rufus and I already ate. You two didn't fix yourself

nothin'?"

"Waitin' on you."

"How bout a chicken sandwich?" Sharon asked. Then, after eight hours in the office and dinner with her oldest son, she went back to work for her other two boys.

Before going to bed, Fuller took the liberty of washing Rufus's wife beater T-shirt. It wasn't really that it stunk, but the guy had been in a bus all night. He washed it by hand in the bathroom sink while Sarah was doing the dishes. He hung it up on the towel rack and thumped his way, bare-chested, chains dangling, back to the kitchen.

"If this little experiment has any positive effect on the boy – the man – in question, you should patent the idea, Lenny," Sarah said.

"Positive? What the hell's that mean? I'm just trying to get the kid to imagine there's more than one way to live."

"That's what I mean. That's positive."

"Actually, sometimes I wonder. Maybe it would – or will – only confuse things. Maybe we should keep the menu simple."

"Maybe. But walking around in somebody else's shoes for a while can't be a bad thing."

"In his case it might get him killed. Sharon says she lives in a pretty tough neighborhood."

Lenny loved Sarah because she was someone he could talk to. The older he got, the fewer interlocutors he had. She was also someone he enjoyed eating with. She was also someone who stiffened his rod and allowed him to float into the powerful male position of post-coital bliss. He gave her similar things, just with different seasoning on them.

The next morning was a Friday and April at its best, cool enough to awaken the skin, but not cold enough to shiver it. The sky was cloudless and when Fuller got out of bed, it was already a block of baby blue. Sarah had left at seven-thirty to teach a class. Lenny put on his costume. He was already used to it. The fact is, he didn't care what he wore. Everything he had was old. He couldn't see any reason to buy anything new. He still looked at people, but they didn't look at him. Except yesterday. Maybe he should go garish, do a Salvador Dali look or something. Old men need to get excessive to keep people looking at them. Did he want people looking at him? Only for pussy. Dali's look had to be for pussy. And money. Fuller didn't care about money. There was nothing he wanted to buy. As long as he had Sarah, he didn't really need pussy. He'd lose Sarah.

When he stopped teaching, who would listen to him? He seduced through his mouth. His ideas had appealed to enough women around campus to have kept him reasonably sexually satisfied. But when he left campus? Would he go gaudy, tawdry? The only real constant he had noticed in his life was his appetite, appetite for food and the female. It hadn't waned in forty years.

He had a cup of coffee and a piece of toast, put on his "do-rag", and pointed his nose out the door into the heart of spring. Rocky Mountain High, he thought as he plodded down the sidewalk looking left, right, up, and out. John Denver finished in the Santa Cruz Bay without a pilot's license. Fish food. Fuller forgot to feed the fish. He back-pedaled, did an inside pivot, and headed back home. As he got to his mailbox he saw a woman with long reddish brown hair hotfooting away from his house, away from him. Had she seen him and run? Was she the borrower of his bed? He couldn't chase her in the boots and he probably wouldn't have chased her anyway.

The fish acted happy to see him. He sprinkled breakfast onto the water and was back out the door.

His journey across campus to his office was without incident other than the fact that, again, people looked at him. He calculated that at least eighty percent of the people he crossed stared at him. He had Rufus's dark glasses on so he could watch them stare without forcing them to avert their glance. He said, "Hi", "Yo", "Whaz happenin", and every now and then a "What it be Daddy" to his passersby. Most smiled, some laughed, others accelerated their gait.

"Yo bro," Sharon said as he walked in the door, "the dean just called. He wants you in the president's office at eleven. He knows you don't have a class this morning. I tried to get you at home before you left."

"Nothing I'd rather do."

"I think you'd better change your clothes."

"No way, baby. A deal's a deal. I promised Rufus that, other than sleeping, I'd wear it until four this afternoon."

"It's your world."

"Maybe not for long. Maybe not this one in any case. What time is it?"

"Ten twenty."

"How's Rufus?"

"Something's going on. When he came in the house last night I could see his eyes water up."

"That's always a good sign."

"How about the wardrobe change?"

"He took a little shit at a gas station which was actually a good thing, I think. It was enough to get him thinking."

"He's a good kid, Sharon. He's got enough of you in him to make it. Where to, I don't know. But he's a damn good kid. Just to do the exchange shows me he's way above most of the pack. What I wonder is what are his alternatives? If he stops his life of crime what could he do? When did he stop school?"

"Dropped out his senior year of high school."

"He could drop back into night school. Maybe he could get into a junior college. They let kids in who can hardly read and write."

"They let 'em in here too if they can shoot a jump shot or tackle somebody in the open field, remember. I'd like to see him get a job. Doing anything. Just something to make him get up in the morning and force him to be somewhere other than in the damn streets."

"You might be right. I don't know why I'm pushing for school. Speaking of which, I'd better go play 'Meet the President'."

"And the Dean..."

"He better be there or it won't be any fun. Adios amiga."

The president's secretary almost peed in her pants when she saw Fuller in his hip-hop getup. Or so it seemed. She could hardly muster a word of reply when

Fuller, removing the shades, said, "Good morning. I was informed that I have a meeting with the president at eleven."

"Y...y...you are?"

"Fuller. Leonard Fuller from the Anthropology Department."

She got up and went down the hall. When she came back she said, "They're waiting to see you," and showed Fuller to the door.

"They" were three, the president, vice president of academic affairs, and the dean of social sciences. They had obviously been warned about his clothing because when he entered the room all three acted as cool as popsicles.

"Have a seat here, Dr. Fuller," the president said.

"Thank you."

"Is your costume for us?"

"No, not at all. I'm trying to get my secretary's son – who just got out of prison – to see the world differently, so we agreed to exchange clothes for twenty-four hours. I don't go back to looking like the other idiot until four this afternoon."

"Thank you for the explanation. We might get back to it later. Dr. Fuller, Dean Jacobs here tells me that you are making derogatory and discriminatory remarks in class about certain religious groups. Is this true?"

"That probably depends on who's listening. I don't really remember what I said. Obviously somebody thought my remarks were derogatory and discriminatory or I wouldn't be here on this glorious spring morning."

"What was the lecture about?"

"Probably about world views, cosmologies, moral beliefs, why people believe what they believe, all that stuff that I think students should think about."

"Did you save your notes from the lecture?"

"Notes? I don't use notes. I've been thinking about this crap for forty years, why would I need notes?"

"Dr. Fuller," the dean snuck in, "would you use a word like 'crap' in a lecture?"

"If I'd use it here, I'd probably use it in a lecture. Wouldn't you think so?"

"Dr. Fuller," the president said retaking the floor, "when you lecture about the things you mentioned before, do you make an effort to be respectful of people's religious orientations?"

Fuller adjusted the "do-rag" which was sliding sideways on his head. "If I remember correctly, I was telling the students that most human beings are sheep. I said that if you look around you, social groups resemble herds of sheep. The hip-hoppers look like the other hip-hoppers. The businessmen look like the other businessmen. The whores look like the other whores. The preachers look like the other preachers. Most people get plopped into a culture and stay in that culture. Most people believe what the culture believes. I think I might also have pointed out that being a sheep is perhaps what most people need because most people don't have the strength or intellect – or whatever it takes – to climb out of the swimming pool they're born into, climb up onto the high dive and dive their own dive. Actually, maybe this is what I was telling Rufus before we changed clothes. I'm not sure."

The three academicians looked at each other. The president spoke, "You didn't answer my question. Are you or are you not respectful of people's religion?"

"It's not their religions I respect. I respect their whole existences. What anthropologist doesn't? I don't respect their religions any more than I respect the kind of toothpaste they use or the brand of underwear they buy. It's all cultural heritage. Cultural baggage. Cultural beauty. Cultural garbage. Just look at you guys, all dressed the same, all using the same kind of language, driving the same kinds of cars, eating in the same kinds of restaurants, drooling over the same kind of women..."

"Dr. Fuller," the president said firmly almost rising

from his chair, "I wouldn't presume and you are straying from the subject."

The vice president of academic affairs was a guy Fuller liked. They had talked before and he had defended Fuller's newspaper article about contemporary Christianity straying lightyears from what Jesus had had to say. He lightened the air. "Maybe we should just stick to your relationship with the students."

"Fine with me. Look gentlemen, I'm paid to teach anthropology. Anthropology reveals the great weight of culture. Religious culture. Moral culture. Metaphysical culture. Scientific culture. Linguistic culture. Family culture. Political culture. Etcetera. Etcetera. I try to get students to understand this as profoundly as possible. I try to get them to see the world as deeply as possible. I try to get them to look into what being a human being is all about. That's all. If I say a Christian is born into a Christian herd and that most Christians are sheep, nothing is more obvious than that. If saying that is disrespectful, then yes, I'm the most disrespectful son of a bitch on campus. If a university student doesn't have the intellectual capacity to realize that most of what he believes is a function of his cultural setting, then our universities are in a pretty sorry state."

"Are you accusing?" the dean said.

"I don't know. Am I? Why did you invite me to this morning tea party? The kids who complained... did you ask them what the lecture was about? Did you think about what I was trying to get across? If you did and don't like the message, then fire me now. Bang, bang. I'd be a happy bird dropping straight to earth. Gentlemen, I don't care. I don't care at all if you ban me from ever standing in front of a class again. If you want to know the truth, you'd probably be doing me a favor. I've enjoyed it here, but the longer I stay, the less time I have to be elsewhere."

"Where might elsewhere be?" the vice president asked.

"Beats me," Fuller said adjusting his pants that, as the conversation wore on, were sliding below the midpoint of his butt. "I might work part time at the Wienerschnitzel. They have great chili-cheese dogs."

"Dr Fuller," the president said, "the accusations brought against you are serious. If they get to me, they're serious. You can't just laugh them off."

"Why not? They're a joke. At a university they're a joke. I wouldn't say that stuff if I was invited to lecture at a synagogue, but this isn't a synagogue, it's supposed to be a place to think and to think profoundly. It's supposed to be an agora for the exchange of ideas.

Gentlemen, men have believed in hundreds of gods and hundreds of different moral Magna Carta. Don't you think students should be aware of the fact that the ones they are floating in might not be airtight. If it might make you feel better, I think I gave atheists a little shit in that lecture, too."

"This is not the locker room," the dean said.

"Do want to get me on the subject of our 'student-athletes', as you call them. Have you ever looked at some of the work your middle linebackers and leading shot blockers do? My kids and yours wrote better in the third grade, and I'm not exaggerating. If you want to talk about that little chapter of campus, I'd love to be part of the conversation."

"That's not what we're here for," the president said firmly. "I think we do, however, need to address the fact that you represent the university and you're walking around campus dressed like a rap singer."

Fuller interrupted. "Whoa... slow down, sir. I don't represent the university and you know it. I don't want to represent anybody. And since when does the institution have a dress code for professors? All I'm trying to do is keep the son of a woman I love out of jail and out of trouble. If wearing the Pope's outfit for a day would keep the kid from messing up, I'd do it. Wouldn't you?"

"I thought you said it was your secretary's son?"

"It is. I love her. She's one of the most wonderful people I know. She should be teaching instead of typing letters. Her mind is as open as..." No usable metaphor popped into his head.

"Doctor Fuller. I am not sure we've gotten anywhere. The dean has handled the complaints as well as he can..."

"The dean has handled the complaints like a boxer who refuses to take off his bathrobe and start the fight. To give in to complaints like this is to perpetuate intellectual vacuity and you know it. Why can't somebody here step out in the ring and put their dukes up."

"Dr. Fuller, it's not as simple as that."

"Oh, it isn't? Letting blind simple-minded religious moles decide what is to be talked about in what is supposed to be a bastion of intellectual curiosity, is like letting six-year-olds run a nuclear power plant." Fuller uncrosses his legs and bends forward. "Actually gentlemen, I might have it all wrong. Sometimes I don't know why I want anybody to think or to question their foundations. In fact the longer I'm around here the less I believe that anybody really thinks. The world just got wound up a few zillion years ago – like one of those rubber-band-powered airplanes we all used to play with as kids – somebody let it go, and this is what it's come to. It doesn't mean any more than that."

"You sound rather deterministic."

"That's because I almost am. If I could get myself to believe in anything it would be that man isn't what he thinks he is. He ain't no freer than a squirrel. He's just bigger and builds different kinds of nests."

There was a pause in the room. The president glanced at the clock on his wall. "If I'm not mistaken, Dr. Fuller, you can retire in one year. Why don't we simply do what we can to avoid controversy until then?"

"I've got a better idea. If you can come up with a pension that pays enough for my goldfish and I to live on, I'll quit next month at the end of the term. You can save some cash, maybe get a few more tutors for the football team or buy new uniforms for the cheerleaders, and I can do something else."

"I'm not sure that's necessary," the vice president offered.

"It's really all right. I've been here a long time. I think it's a good time to go."

The president rose from his chair followed by the two other men. Fuller followed suit, struggling to keep his pants from falling to his knees.

"I think we've hit enough sides of the issue. I'll get

back to you next week, Dr. Fuller," the president said.

"I'll quit right now if you want."

"I'll be in touch next week."

Fuller shook everybody's hand. He put on Rufus's shades. The clock on the president's wall said eleven forty. The beautiful April morning was still alive. The three escorted Fuller to the door. He gave them a little thumbs up and shuffled past the secretary's desk.

12

"Dolores just called," Sharon said when he got to the office.

"What about?"

"She didn't say. She seemed happy though."

"Glad to hear it."

"How'd it go with the president?"

"We might be getting a divorce."

"Who's 'we'?"

"The school and I."

"You wouldn't do that to me?"

"I've only got one more year anyway. We might as well chop it down to size. When I go you'll meet some nice young Harvard graduate with blonde hair, blue eyes, and lips you can't resist."

"What happened?"

"I told them I'd quit today. He said he'd call me next week."

Sharon rose from her chair like a dinosaur from the sea and came over and hugged Fuller. In her arms he was a doll. She smelled good. For an instant Fuller wondered why they hadn't ever gotten romantic. She kissed the side of his head. The referee of time unclenched them.

"I've got a class, so if Rufus comes, tell him I haven't run off to Motown?"

"Will do, honey. Thanks for talking with him and making a fool out of yourself."

"No more of a fool than usual."

"True."

"Let me give Dolores a quick call." He went to his office and dialed his ex-wife's number.

"Hello."

"What's up sweetheart?"

"Lenny."

"Still."

"Lenny, I just wanted to tell you I moved out."

"You left the man you left me for?"

"Just like turning in a used car."

"Where'd you move into?"

"The Saab."

"It's got bad toilet facilities."

"It's only temporary."

"I'm going to see Laurie in a couple hours. She thinks she's pregnant."

"It's about time she and that physicist fused."

"I'm driving."

"Alone?"

"I'm a big girl."

"Be careful. Remember to stop when you get to Oregon. There's an ocean out there."

"Very funny. Anyway, after that I might go down to California and see Carrie. For the first time in twenty-eight years, I'm free."

"Do your thing. Is the car running okay?"

"Seems to be. Arthur took care of it all these years. He says it's a collector's item."

"So are you. Listen, I've got to go teach a class. Give everybody a kiss."

"Goodbye darling." The phone clicked. This conversation ended as abruptly as the one with the president had. Fuller had always been fascinated by how such moments end. One minute you're in the middle of something, the next minute you and the coffee stain have been wiped clean from the table.

He tromped to class. He would give one lecture in his Eminem outfit. The students would remember it more than any other. He would briefly explain why he was dressed the way he was, then he would talk about the pluses and minuses of stepping out of one's culture. Was it in invitation to insanity? Was it possible to ever really step out? If one stepped out, would one automatically step into another one? Was it possible to live outside of culture. Was it possible to put one's culture in brackets, live away from it, then crawl back into it? Is that what Oscar Wilde did when he called a priest to his death bed in the little room off the Rue de Seine in Paris? Was it even possible to separate a man from his culture? Was the idea, that a man is an entity and his culture a separate entity, a myth? Is it possible to remove all myth from a civilization? What would be left? Is kinship a myth? Is love a myth? Is success a myth? Is education a myth? Is the world a great machine that spins so fast that nothing can escape its innate forces? If God is a myth, if man is not the son of God, what is he? If evolution is a myth, if man is not the fruit of evolution, what is he? What other possibilities are there? To have only two is a rather meager choice. Is the world a mystery far beyond the reach of man? Is man a mystery far beyond the reach of the world?

Fuller had fun. He walked around the room as he spoke. Forty-five minutes of the hip-hop strut mixed with a professor's extemporaneous academic rap. Fuller decided to end with a little rhyme:

So who's the man
The man with the plan?
We anthros supposed to know
Supposed to say how it's so

But we in the dark
Like every other shark
The only thing for sure
Is that there ain't no cure

Eat or be eaten, the Big Man say
It's the only game we all really play
So dig the circus while the tent is up
Drink all you can from life's cup

Maybe we ain't free
Don't choose who we ever be
If we take a good peep
The shit's pretty deep

Deeper than you or I will ever know

A few of the students clapped when he finished. He took off the "do-rag", curtsied, waved goodbye, and walked out the door. Professor Lenny Fuller had given his last lecture.

13

Rufus was talking to his mother when Fuller got to the office. His hair was symmetrically buffed up and he looked like a Harvard law student or maybe a real estate salesman in Chicago. Fuller gave him a hug and sat down next to him.

"How'd class go?" Sharon asked.

"I finished with an ad lib rap. It was probably the most pleasurable lesson I've had since a student named Anne hinted I was the sexiest guy on campus about twenty-eight years ago one day after class."

"You rapped?" Rufus grinned. "Lemme hear it."

"If I could remember it I'd copyright it. I was mostly concentrating on the rhyme. Do those guys memorize the words or do they make it up as they go along? If they make it up, I'll reconsider my summary judgment that they are talentless charlatans. It wasn't easy to come up with five verses on the run. I did make sure I got the word 'bitch' in there. The last line went something like 'So kiss the bitch while you can / Before you know it she's up and ran'. In this case the bitch was life itself, which may not have been clear to my audience. I made sure that when I said 'bitch' I had my lips as far forward as possible. Give me a few months and I might have an act down. How'd it go for you Rufus? It's almost four o'clock. Time to put your chains back on."

"Very funny," Rufus smiled. "I got one thing to say about wearin' your shit. It smell good. What kind a detergent you use?"

"I buy whatever's on sale. I can't remember what it is. I'll check though for you."

"I liked yo shoes. The pants is cool, too, but you ain't got enough pockets to hide your drugs and knives and shit."

"I see what you mean," Fuller said. "How'd you like the corduroy material? It's not real popular in your neck of the woods, I don't think."

"I gotta hand it to you there. Shit a lot softer than my jeans. I should start a new style. Jeans made outta the corduroy crap. The bitches might start puttin' their hands..."

"Rufus!" Sharon jumped in.

"Come on Mom, the Doc and I's only talkin' shit. But I'll be honest with you Doc, you right about one thing."

"What's that?" Sharon asked anxious to hear something half serious come out of her son's mouth.

"People did look at me different."

"Did you look at them different?" Fuller asked.

"Not at first, but today I did. They didn't look so much like the enemy no more."

"Praise the Lawd!" Sharon said. "My boy's been saved!" Sharon howled and laughed. "The war is over! Bring out the white flags and the doves!"

"Not so fast Momma," Fuller said. "The man ain't finished talkin'."

"Let's just say this," Rufus said, "if I hadda wear your shit another day or two, it wouldn't be no big deal. As long as I stay outta Momma's gas stations."

"That's kind of the way I feel," Fuller said. "Only in my case, I gotta stay out of the president's office."

"You two sound like cute little blood brothers," Sharon offered.

"Why don't Rufus and I change clothes and you two

come over to my house for dinner. It's Friday night. I'm as free as my goldfish. Besides, I want Rufus to hear some of my music."

"D'you listen to mine?"

"Hell, yes. For about thirty seconds. So you've got to listen to mine for thirty seconds, then we're even. I'll nail you with some Bizet. 'The Pearl Fishermen'. A hell of an opera. Two guys love the same bitch. Thirty seconds of that, Rufus, and you be messed up."

"It free food, Momma," Rufus said. "You promise ony thirty seconds uh da music?"

"Done deal."

"Dr. Fuller," Sharon said, "do you realize I've never been to my boss's house."

"Then let him sin no more," Fuller said. "Let him integrate the damn neighborhood tonight. There are blonds, brunettes, grey old men, reddish-brown heads, goldfish, German Shepherds, squirrels, blackbirds, dental assistants, and cockroaches. We might as well bring some Juppitts in."

Rufus and Fuller went to his office and put their respective clothes back on. Rufus put the "do-rag" in the jacket pocket with the Sony machine. They locked up the office and drove to Fuller's house in Sharon's car. It had a strange smell, Fuller thought, like hot dogs and cotton candy. Naturally, after a minute or two he couldn't smell it anymore.

When they pulled into the empty driveway, Fuller knew something was up because the curtains in the front room were drawn. He never closed them.

"Any bets on who's been in my bed?" he asked.

"What the man talkin' about?" Rufus said from the back seat.

"He finds long brown hairs in his bed," Sharon said.

"Reddish-brown," Fuller corrected. "Long reddish-brown. Very pretty, in fact."

When they got to the front door and Fuller opened it without a key, Rufus said, "Maybe you should start usin' da lock, Doc."

"Maybe people should stop borrowing my bed without asking. Listen, they left the radio on again."

"Who's they?" Sharon said.

"Whoever the reddish brunette is carousing with. They always set the clock radio and forget to turn it off."

"Maybe they ain't forgettin'," Rufus said. "Maybe they want ya to know they been around."

"Maybe you're right. Take your coats off," Fuller said.

"But really, Doc, why don't you lock yo fuckin' door?" Rufus said slipping off his mammoth jacket.

"I hate keys and there's nothing to steal. Keys are a

constant reminder of how many dishonest characters there are in the world. Do you realize that the only reason a key exists is because people take what doesn't belong to them? If there were no thieves, there would be no keys. Some anthropologist should write a book on the history and evolution of keys." He shows them into the living room. "I'll be right back. I'm just going to check the bedroom."

The radio was set for four again. He pulled back the covers and there, laying vertically on the white pillowcase, glimmering like a soft neon light, was the third mystic strand. Fuller took it to the bathroom and set it on the towel with the other two.

"That makes three," he said returning to the living room. "Three gorgeous, luscious hairs found by detective Lenny Fuller in his own bed. No other evidence of foul or fair play. Just the hair and the radio on."

"Maybe you should call the police," his secretary said.

"I'm having too much fun," Fuller said.

"As long as they ain't stealin' your shit," Rufus said as he was flipping through Fuller's collection of records. "What'd you say you was goin' to play for me? Summin' about fishin'?"

"Now's as good a time as any. It's an opera. I'll put on my favorite part, a male duet by two men in love with the same woman. You can stop it after thirty seconds if you want to. No cheating. What can I get you to drink?"

"Beer."

"Beer."

Fuller put the music on and went to the kitchen. He emptied a bag of taco chips into a bowl and grabbed three beers and a jar of salsa out of the fridge. When he came back to his guests the music was still on. "You're a better man than I, Rufus."

"Hey, you probably already heard fuckin' rap. I ain't never heard no shit like this before."

"You have to acquire a taste for it, don't you think?" Sharon said.

"Maybe Rufus would say the same thing about rap music."

"Wouldn't know. I don't know nothin' else."

"I'll vouch for that," his mother says.

"My father used to listen to opera and I hated it," Fuller says. "Then slowly but surely I got hooked."

"Kinda like crack, uh Doc?"

"That's one I wouldn't know. So what shall we feast on to celebrate the Great Exchange of Clothes and Rufus's return to the Great Rocky Mountains? How about if I make a salad and order some pizza?"

Everybody agreed. Bizet's opera quietly extinguished

itself while Fuller was making the salad in the kitchen. The pizza arrived. They supped like kings and queen. Into their third round of beers, Fuller asked Rufus if he lifted a lot of weights in prison. Rufus said the weights had lifted him out of eternal boredom. Fuller and Sharon were quite sure that behind those chains and tattoo fields something was happening.

14

It was Monday morning, the twenty-seventh of April. The word "bitch" had done it. A student had called a parent, the parent called the dean, the dean called the president. The president didn't bother to call the vice president of academic affairs. Fuller was fired.

Sharon gave him the letter when he walked in the door at nine thirty. He knew by looking at the return address. He read it quickly, smiled, and said, "Juan José, the gardener, is supposed to be here at ten. I'll be in my office. Have you got any boxes? I've got a few things I want to keep. Otherwise we'll just give the stuff away to whoever wants it. I'll try to find a couple of good books for your son."

"Lenny," Sharon said, her face glittering with tears, "you don't mean it...?"

"They mean it. 'Immediate termination of all activity associated with the university'."

Sharon threw her bare bear arms around him and almost crushed him. This squeezed a drop or two from his eyes. They stayed embraced until the door opened. The gardener was early.

"I don't want to be late for the professor," he said sheepishly.

"You couldn't have come at a better time," Fuller said not going into details. "We'll go back to my house right now. I was going to take you there just before lunch, but we can go now. Sharon, after Juan José gets set up, I'll come back to the office. I'd say around eleven, eleven thirty. If anybody calls tell them to start designing a statue of me to be put the west entrance to campus. I won't accept anything less than fifteen feet high. They can plant it next to the waterfall."

Walking back across the school with the gardener was like watching a fashion show with Hugh Hefner; all the flowers and bushes stood out. Fuller's eyes took in double or triple of what they had seen a half hour earlier on his way to the office. Normally he saw primarily people, with a few wandering glances at the botany.

With Juan José at his side, he saw a blooming orgy of pinks, purples, yellows, oranges, and greens. "You guys do good work," he said.

"Glad somebody notice."

At ten fifteen they were at the house.

"Coffee or anything?"

"No gracias. All that done."

They went straight to the bedroom.

"All right Juan, here's the deal. You're going to stay under this bed until I come home this afternoon at around four o'clock. I've put a bottle of water under there for you, a sandwich, an apple, and a bag of cookies. Do you need anything else?" The gardener shook his head. "Just don't eat if anybody comes. If you have to go to the toilet, go. But again, don't go if anybody's in the house. If you go, go fast and get right back under the bed. If somebody comes, you don't make a sound and try to remember everything you hear. Try to get a good look at any shoes you see walking across the bedroom. Fifteen dollars an hour. I'll pay you when I get back. I've put a little pillow under there for you. Okay? Got it?"

"I got it," Juan said. "I start new detective career."

He was small and thin and it was easy for him to fit under the bed. Fuller kneeled down to be sure everything was okay, waved goodbye, then made his third trip across campus on this morning of his last day after twenty-nine years at the university. He detoured to Safeway to pick up two medium-sized cardboard boxes.

Sarah was waiting for him in his office. "So they finally weeded out the garden. Finally threw out the trash. Finally took measures to stop corrupting the youth of America. Finally gave my darling boyfriend a much-deserved vacation." She had had time to think about what she was going to say first to her dethroned part-time pal.

"News travels quickly as we approach the twenty-first century."

"I've got extrasensory conception."

"How did they count time before Jesus came along? I can't remember. Maybe they were smart enough not to count. When you think about it for two seconds, man is so absurdly anthropomorphically small when it comes to talking about time. For all we know, ninety-nine tillion zillion years ago there were civilizations traipsing around the globe. And ninety-nine zillion years before them maybe there was another crew. Our profundity in thinking about time is about as deep as a strawberry milkshake."

"I thought you got fired, professor. Actually I stopped by to invite you out to lunch."

"You can still invite me out to lunch. I can't go home until four o'clock. I've got my place staked out. Juan José, my gardener friend, is going to solve the great mystery of who is slipping between my sheets." He put the boxes on the floor and started looking through his books. "If you want, you can start helping me pack. I think the powers that be have given me a twelve noon check-out time."

"So what tipped the iceberg? What happened?"

"Sharon didn't tell you?"

"Not the details."

"As you remember, on Thursday I changed clothes with her son, Rufus, the one who recently was released from one of our nation's fine detention centers. Friday morning they – the president, dean and vice president – called me in and I was still wearing his stuff, you know, the baggy jeans, the 'do-rag', the chains... the whole bit. Then that afternoon I gave a lecture in the outfit that I finished with a rap song. Somebody complained. The last straw, I guess. Actually, they're just doing me a favor."

"You did a rap song?"

"I made it up. I even used a ruler for a microphone that I held sideways like the Puffy Daddies do. I did the shuffle, too."

"Fortunately they fired you before you did Britney Spears and Madonna."

"You be right, baby. Now hepp me clean dis shit out."

It was done in an hour. Fuller gave Sharon half a dozen books for Rufus and a couple of his old articles, one about the idiocy of the word "race", and another about how race is nothing and culture is everything. He kept the Navajo rug and the picture of the weaver in the Utah desert. The books he saved were mostly Sarah's choices. He gave Sharon his last stack of corrected tests, all A+ except for the middle linebacker's delicious B+. They put the boxes in Sarah's car. Fuller came back to kiss Sharon.

"Tell Rufus to give me a call or stop by the house whenever he wants to. Maybe he and I should start a new fashion line where we blend hip-hop and Ralph Lauren."

"I think it's already happening. They dress people in anything to make a buck. Worst of it is, they get them fools to all be thinkin' they look good."

"Oh well. Listen, I'd better stay off campus for a while, so we'll meet at Tia Maria's or something."

"You're on professor. My calendar is as open as the Red Sea."

"Bye Sharon."

"Bye Lenny."

"You're the best."

Their lips brushed as Fuller's head went from her right ear, across her face, to her left ear.

15

Sarah and Fuller pulled into his driveway a few minutes after four.

"Come on in," Fuller said. "Help me solve the riddle."

The door was ajar and the radio was on. "We're in business," he said. "I just hope Juan José is still alive." They walked stealthily down the hall toward the bedroom. The bedding was definitely not the way Fuller had left it that morning. He kneeled down and looked for the gardener. He was not there. His sandwich was eaten, the cookie bag had been opened, and the bottle of water and pillow were there. But there was no Juan José Carlos Rodriguez.

"He's gone."

"Are you sure he knew he was supposed to stay until you got back?"

"Sure I'm sure. I told him I'd be back at four." Fuller stood up and examined the sheets with Sarah. There was more than one hair. There were five or six of them. All reddish-brown. All long.

"I'll be damned," Sarah said.

"I'll be god damned," Fuller said. "I'm going to go see if I can call Juan José. He should have a telephone." He went to the living room while Sarah took a peek under the bed and cleaned up the gardener's lunch. While Fuller was thumbing through the phone book, there was a soft knock on the door. Fuller opened it slowly. It was the gardener looking as anxious as a cow near the front of the line in a slaughterhouse.

"I'm sorry professor. I get too scared. I run away. But I don't go home. I wait outside for you. I see the car in the driveway and I come back." He was breathing heavily.

Sarah came in from the bedroom and they all sat down in the living room. "This is Sarah Fletcher, Juan."

"Buenos dias."

"What scared you, Juan? What did you see? What did you hear?" Fuller said trying to leave things as open as possible."

"I wait for a long time, maybe two hours. I don't have a watch. Then I hear footsteps coming down the hall. Sound like boots. I see the bedroom door move and shiny black boots come in."

"A man or a woman?"

"Woman. I'm sure. She sits on the bed and I see boots drop to the floor. Then she stand up and clothes start falling, too. Sweater, skirt, stocking, brassiere, underpants... everything she have on, I think. Then she lie in the bed and do nothing for a few minutes. Then, suddenly, I hear man's voice. Deep, loud voice. He say, 'READY OR NOT, HERE I COME'."

"He said, 'Ready or not, here I come?' Are you sure?"

"Sure."

Did the voice come from the hallway?"

"No. This the scary part. Nobody come through the door. I don't see any more feet or shoes. Then the voice sounds like it's on top of me in the bed. It starts saying that the woman she looks so beautiful, so beautiful, as if Botta... Bowla... something... as beautiful as if a Bowlacherry or somebody made her. Then he say something about Virgin Mary and immaculate conception."

"What?"

"I listen hard. He talk about virgins and stuff like that being for the birds."

"Virgins being for the birds?" Fuller says, and Sarah breaks out laughing.

"He's right about that," she says. "But who is *he*?"

"This why I get scared. I think *who is he*? Who is he who is talking who didn't walk in through the door? Then he say something about time being of the essence. He say they can't wait much longer because the baby need to come by the year 2000."

"Juan, are you sure about all this?" Fuller says.

"Professor, I do just what you tell me. I get nervous, but I do what you tell me."

"Okay, then what happened?"

"He say again that they can't waste any more time and that virgin stuff and immaculate conception not working. He say they need to try other way."

"Did the woman say anything?"

"Not much. Very little. She seem to be rolling around a little while they talk, but I not sure if it he or she rolling around."

"And then...?"

"So he say they try other method and then he start whispering and laughing a little. Then she start laughing and the next thing you know I think the bed going to fall on my head and kill me. She start screaming and he start screaming and she saying *O MY GOD, O MY GOD* and he saying *O JULIA, O JULIA...*"

"You sure he called her 'Julia'?"

Juan looked at Fuller with a tired drawn face. His brow was damp. He squirmed. "Professor, I promise you I tell you right. I know you think I'm crazy. This part of the reason I get afraid. I think the professor going to think me crazy as a fruitcake. But I tell you *la verdad*. I tell you what I hear."

"Was the radio on? Are you sure the voices weren't coming out of the radio?"

"How can I be sure? I under the bed. But I don't think so. I don't hear anybody fooling with buttons on the radio."

"So then what happened?"

"When they finish screaming and making me think the bed going to fall, things get very quiet for a few minutes, then the big voice says, *IF THAT DOESN'T DO IT NOTHING WILL*. Then he say something about the girl having a little sleep and that he got to go. Then he start talking about you, professor, and he say you be home around four. Then I hear what sound like somebody touching the buttons on the radio clock. Then the big voice say *I'LL STAY IN TOUCH* and I don't hear it anymore."

Sarah and Fuller look at each other and smile. Fuller goes to the kitchen and brings back an opened bottle of Chardonnay and three glasses. He pours everybody a drink. "Cheers," he says. "Juan you've done a great job. You've earned your money. It sounds to me like history is going to take a new turn. What do you think, Sarah?"

"Things might be a little more fun this time around."

"What do you think, Juan. What do you make of it all?"

The gardener takes a sip of his wine, rubs his forehead, then says half smiling, "I don't know, professor. You the anthropologist."

BOOKS BY JON FERGUSON

(Published by Huge Jam, 2022)

Adam's Cane
Foster's Depression
The Last Day Forever
Jesus & Mary
Mary & God
God & Naomi
The Flood
The Anthropologist
Three Forgotten Tales

Out soon by the same author:

Nietzsche for Breakfast
The Old Man and the Stone
Don't Bullshit Me Daddy

www.hugejam.com
www.jonfergusonbooks.com

ABOUT THE AUTHOR

Jon Ferguson was born in October 1949 in Oakland, California, into a devout Christian family, much like his favorite philosopher, Friedrich Nietzsche. In fact, as a child, church services were held in the family living room. At age 17, his passion for sport was almost usurped by a keenness to save the world when he enrolled at the Mormon-owned Brigham Young University. Little by little, though, he realized that if Jesus couldn't do it, neither could he. His faith in divinity began to crumble. With an adieu to the US academic world where he'd been immersed in anthropology and philosophy – and with a desire to engage with the world at large – Ferguson hopped on a plane in 1973 and by chance ended up in Nyon, Switzerland where he was soon playing basketball in the top Swiss league, becoming a key player in what fans consider to have been the golden age.

Half a century later, still in Switzerland, he is now just as well known for his writing (eighteen books published in French) as for his coaching (thirty years' worth). He won more games than any coach in Swiss basketball history, but he likes to remind people that he lost more than everyone else as well... He has written over twenty novels and a book on Nietzsche, Nietzsche au Petit Déjeuner ("Nietzsche for Breakfast") and a book on the history of Swiss basketball, Of Hoops and Men. For twenty-five years he also wrote a bi-weekly column in the Lausanne newspaper called "Ainsi Parla Schmaltz". His novel Farley's Jewel (Cinco Puntos Press, 1998) won a Barnes & Noble "Discover Great New Writers of America" prize.

Find out more:
www.jonfergusonbooks.com